ALL THAT I HAVE

ALL THAT I HAVE

A NOVEL

Castle Freeman Jr.

Duckworth Overlook

First published in the United Kingdom by Duckworth in 2010

Duckworth, an imprint of Prelude Books Ltd
13 Carrington Road, Richmond,
TW10 5AA, United Kingdom
www.preludebooks.co.uk

For bulk and special sales please contact
info@preludebooks.co.uk

A catalogue record for this book is available from the British Library.

Printed in the UK by Clays Ltd, Elcograf S.p.A.

978-0-7156-3902-3

3 5 7 9 10 8 6 4

And he answering said to his father,
Lo, these many years do I serve thee,
neither transgressed I at any time thy
commandment: and yet thou never
gavest me a kid, that I might make
merry with my friends: But as soon as
thy son was come, which hath devoured
thy living with harlots, thou hast killed
for him the fatted calf. And he said unto
him, Son, thou art ever with me, and
all that I have is thine.

The Gospel according to St. Luke, 15:29–31

CONTENTS

THE NEW MALE AND
THE MORNING BACK

Sharp at seven Tuesday morning, Clemmie, barefoot in her robe, was standing at the kitchen counter putting cream in her coffee when the squawker went. Clemmie listened. She took a sip of coffee. The squawker quit. Clemmie turned from the counter.

"What's a new male?" she asked.

I was sitting at the breakfast table, behind Clemmie. I was looking at her back. Her morning back. We'd had another of our little go-rounds the night before, nothing too serious: a club match, an exhibition. Still, this morning here I was looking at her back. When she wants to, Clemmie can show you a back like the north side of Mount Nebo.

It was Trooper Timberlake on the squawker, from someplace way to hell and gone out on the Diamond Mountain road in Ulster. He sounded puzzled.

"That was young Timberlake," I said. "I'd better go."

"He said a new male, though," Clemmie said. "What did he mean? What's a new male?"

"I am," I said. "I'm a new male. You didn't know that?"

"Sure, you are," said Clemmie.

That sounded pretty good, I thought. If I can get the door open that far, I can get her to come through it. I thought I'd try to push it for another inch.

"There's a new kind of male," I said. "I'm one of them. One of him."

"If that's so," said Clemmie, "then things are worse than anybody knew."

There she was. She's back on the premises, it looks like, back on the reservation — or soon will be. I drank my coffee and got up from the table.

"I'd better go ahead," I said.

"Have some breakfast first," said Clemmie. "Have some toast."

"The new male don't eat breakfast," I said. I went to the kitchen door and got the truck keys from their hook.

"But, really," said Clemmie, "he did say something about a new male, didn't he? What did he mean?"

"I don't think that's what he said," I told her.

———

Trooper Timberlake was in the turnout for the snowplows right at the Ulster town line. I pulled the truck in behind him. I could see he had somebody in the rear of the patrol car, behind the grill. Timberlake left the patrol car and came back to me.

Timberlake was probably twenty-five. He had the state police thing about down: six-four or -five, blond, fit, head cropped so close it was nearly shaved. He looked like the world's largest baby, a baby who had come out of his mother's belly doing one-arm pushups. Timberlake had come to the state police from the Marine Corps. A lot of them did at the state police. You don't have to be General Patton come back from the dead to rise in that organization, but it don't hurt you if you are.

"Subject's been in a fight, Sheriff," Timberlake said. "Somebody driving by found him, called it in. He was tied to a tree over there. He's got a bump on his head, got a big shiner, and plus his arm's hurt somehow. Ambulance is en route."

"Good morning to you, too, Trooper," I said.

"Can't get much out of him," Timberlake went on. "One thing: he's not from around here. He can't even speak English — can't or won't. Yelling and carrying on in some language I can't make anything of. Some garbage."

"No clothes?"

"That's affirmative, Sheriff. Not a patch on him."

"Tied to a tree?"

"That's affirmative, Sheriff. Tied to a tree, shit beat out him, and raving butt naked."

"Let's have a look at him," I said.

Timberlake stepped away, and I got down from the truck. The two of us went up to Timberlake's patrol car and the man sitting in the rear.

"Best keep back a little, Sheriff," said Timberlake.

The man in the patrol car was handcuffed behind his back. He had a blanket wrapped around his shoulders, the ends folded across his lap. He was short and skinny. He had long greasy blond hair and skin that was too white, as though he lived in your cellar or at the bottom of your well. He wore no clothes, nothing, not even his socks. When Timberlake and I came up to the patrol car, he turned his head and spat toward us out the half-open window.

"He spits, Sheriff," said Timberlake.

The naked man commenced to thrash around and kick the seat in front of him. He beat his head against the window glass. He shouted and cursed at us. Whatever language he was speaking sounded like you're going through a big log of rock maple with a chain saw and you hit an old iron sugar tap in there.

"What's that he's talking, Sheriff?" Timberlake asked.

"That's Russian," I said.

"Russian?"

"Sure," I said. "Don't you know Russian when you hear it, Trooper?"

"Negative, Sheriff," said Timberlake.

"I thought they trained you kids today," I said.

"Come on, Sheriff," said Timberlake.

"Who did you say called it in?"

"I couldn't say, Sheriff. They didn't leave a name."

"Here's your medics," I said.

The ambulance from Cumberland drove up, and the medical team piled out and came over to the patrol car. They took one look at Trooper Timberlake's passenger, yelling nobody knew what at them and kicking and spitting and snapping like a snake in the back of the patrol car, and refused to go anywhere near him. But the driver was a big strong fellow, and Timberlake was another, and between the three of us we managed to get a bag on the Russian's head and wrestle him out of the car. Even so, we almost lost him when he head-butted the ambulance driver, kicked Timberlake where you don't want to be kicked, and took off running full tilt for the road. He had to get past me, though, and as he tried to do that I sidestepped and stuck out my foot. The Russian tripped and went down hard on his face, with Timberlake and the driver right on top of him, neither of them feeling too kindly toward him anymore. They got him onto a stretcher, got him strapped down good and tight. Then we shoved him into the ambulance. They took him to Brattleboro. Timberlake's barracks commander thought the International School down there might have somebody who could talk to him.

———

The thing is, Clemmie says I don't like her father. She's right: I don't. He don't like me either, though, so that's okay, we're even.

You don't have to like your wife's father. He don't have to like you. It's not a problem, really, but Clemmie sees it as one. And then, she says I don't like her father *and never have*. That's not right. I did like him. I liked him fine for five, ten minutes after the two of us were introduced by Clemmie. It took me that long to figure out that Addison Jessup didn't approve of me, didn't think I was anywhere near good enough for his only daughter, didn't like the idea of her taking up with a half-assed woodchuck cop — didn't like much of anything about Clemmie and me.

The fact that the week before we met I had busted Addison for driving under the influence probably didn't help us get along real smooth. But there again, it didn't have to have been a problem. It wasn't for me. The sheriff's department is different from other law enforcement work in some ways, as I will explain by and by, but it's like all the rest in this: the people want you to do your job, and they want you not to do your job. They want you to do your job, but not on them.

"If you could just make a little bit of an effort with him," Clemmie said. "If you could, just once, meet him halfway. He's not young, you know. His health isn't great. He won't be around forever."

"He won't?" I asked her. "Are you sure?"

"I can't be on your side and on his side, too," Clemmie said. "I'm right in the middle here all the time."

"You ain't in the middle of nothing," I said. "I'm the illiterate redneck that's putting the blocks to your dad's only daughter, his little girl. He don't like that. I can't make him like it. You can't. Quit worrying about it."

"He doesn't think you're an illiterate redneck."

"Sure, he does. He's right, too."

"If he's right, then what does that make me?"

"The wife of an illiterate redneck, it looks like."

"Exactly. You see? You don't think about that."

"Don't I?"

"No. You don't. Never. You just go ahead the way you do, the way you always have. You're that sure. You don't see me."

"I see you fine."

"You don't. You don't see me. You don't see anyone."

"I see you. I see your dad. You want to know what I see?"

"No. Forget it."

"You want to know?"

"Just forget it."

"I'll tell you if you want to know."

"I don't want to know. My Lord. You know what I want? What I'd like? I'd like to be like you. Don't laugh: I really would. Calm. Sure. Mister Law. That would be great. I'd love that. I really would. How do you do it? How do you get that way?"

"I took a course."

I slept on the couch that night, and then the next day I got the morning back from Clemmie. Naturally, I got it. If I hadn't, I would have worried. I would have missed the back. How Addison felt about me, how I felt about Addison, what it all meant to Clemmie, what it meant to me, how it all went round and round, was the gift that keeps on giving to Clemmie and me. We had hunted those woods many a time and left behind a lot of fur and feathers and a lot of spent brass.

But joy cometh in the morning, as they used to say in church — and if it don't, at least you can get out of the house and go to work. Thank God for the new male.

2

THE RUSSIANS AT DISNEYLAND

Do I know Russian?

I do not, no more than Trooper Timberlake does. 'Course I don't. With my crack about how he hadn't been trained right and I had, I was taking a little shot at Timberlake. I was sticking it to him, a little. Sure, I was. With the Timberlakes of this world, you almost have to stick it to them when you can, don't you? Timberlake don't mind. He's — what are you when you're padded all around, when they can't get to you? He's invulnerable. Taking a little shot at Timberlake is like shooting an elephant in the hindquarters with a BB gun: not only is he not hurt, you can't tell for sure whether he knows he's been hit.

So no, I didn't know Russian was what Timberlake's under-dressed customer was talking up on Diamond Mountain. I didn't know, but I did. Because as soon as Timberlake had asked me what the fellow was talking and I'd heard myself say Russian, I knew I was right, and I knew why. A wire had arced to another wire in a different part of the panel, and a whole new section of the board had lit up. A Russian. A naked Russian. Another naked Russian.

———

It was the Friday before Timberlake's Russian turned up that we had responded to an automatic alarm from a vacation place in Grenada. The alarm was relayed from a private security company I'd never heard of. That wasn't unusual. A good many of the newer properties contracted for surveillance and security service with outfits in all kinds of places; in fact, it seemed as though the bigger and fancier the house, the farther away its security was apt to be.

The house this alarm had come from was most of an hour's drive from the sheriff's department, but one of my deputies, Deputy Keen, was patrolling in Grenada that morning, so I had Beverly, our dispatcher, get him on the radio and tell him to take the call. I went back to work. I had a stiff letter that morning from the first selectman in Ambrose. It had come to his attention that one of my deputies, in apprehending a speeder in his town, had pursued the violator for one-half mile into the neighboring town of Gilead. Why, the selectman wanted to know, was the entire pursuit charged against Ambrose's contract with the sheriff's department? Why couldn't Gilead pay its fair share of the charges incurred in this action? Did I not realize that the funds I expended came out of the pockets of overburdened property taxpayers? Did I not understand the need for the strictest accounting and over-sight of the monies entrusted to me? Was I not little more than an embezzler, little better than a pirate? If you're the sheriff, you get letters like this one, and if you want to go on being the sheriff, you answer them. But they can grind you down, no question.

Half an hour later, Beverly called me from her desk. "It's Lyle," she said. "Can you talk to him?"

I got on the radio. "Deputy?" I said.

"Sheriff?" said Deputy Keen. He sounded like he couldn't hear me well. Our radios are US military surplus, from the Army of the Potomac.

"I hear you fine, Deputy," I said.

"Can you get up here?" the deputy asked. "I'm at the auto-alarm in Grenada."

"What have you got?"

"Break-in," said Keen. "Can you get up here? You might want to have a look."

"What for?" I asked him. "Was somebody in the place?"

"Nope. Place is empty. They have a caretaker. I called him. He's on his way. Can you get up here?"

"Why?"

"Your boy's been working," said Lyle. "You might want to see for yourself."

"My boy?"

"I'd guess so," said the deputy. "I'll show you. See what you think."

Deputy Keen gave me directions, and I set out about eleven. I cranked the truck right up and used the blue light. "My boy," the deputy had said. I knew who he meant.

———

When I turned off the falls road in Grenada and took the old stage road that goes back into the hills, I realized that the place I was going to must be Disneyland.

Driving at night on the highway that takes you under Stratton Mountain and south toward the valley, you see, as you come over a hill, a brightly lit house far off to your right, to the west, on top of the ridge. Whosever place it is, they must own stock in the power company, you think, because they've got not only inside lights, but yard lights, spotlights, floodlights. They've got the whole light store up there. Standing all alone on top of its ridge in the darkness, the place looked like a night game at Fenway Park. People around here called it Disneyland.

I found the driveway to the house five miles up the stage road. There was a gate, the kind you see at a railway crossing: a single bar swung up and down from one end by an electric control on the gatepost. The gate was up. Whoever raised it had known the code you had to punch into the panel on the post to work the gate. Some owners of vacation places give their security codes to the sheriff's department, to the local fire department, but we didn't have a code on file for this place, never had. As I went through the gate and up the drive, I thought about that.

It was quite a driveway. It went up the hill through the woods in a bend, then down, over a brook on a concrete bridge, and up some more. I remembered Beverly saying that driveway was just short of a quarter-mile long. Her son-in-law worked for the excavator who had put it in. I once asked Beverly if he'd told her what the sticker was on a quarter-mile driveway with a bridge to it. She said yes, he had. I asked her for the number, but she wouldn't give it to me. You're my boss, said Beverly. If I told you, you'd think I was a liar or been drinking or both. You'd have to fire me.

The drive ended in a circle in front of the house. The house was, after that approach, a disappointment for a minute. Only for a minute. It was made of glass and some dark wood, and though it didn't seem to have a full second story, it had any amount of towers, peaks, balconies, porches, and bays. I mean, the place went on and on.

Deputy Keen's patrol car was parked in the circle. He came out of the house as I was leaving the truck. Keen was by himself.

"Caretaker not here yet?" I asked him.

"Not yet," said the deputy.

We started for the house, walking side by side.

"Gate was open," Keen said. He had his head turned and was looking at me.

"Yes, it was," I said.

"What's that tell you?"

"Where's the break-in?" I asked him.

"Around back," said Keen. "It's an easy one."

"An easy one?"

"Easy as pie, Sheriff," said Deputy Keen.

He led the way around the house and onto a deep porch that went along the rear of the building and overlooked a lawn that must have covered five acres, sloping down from the house to woods in the distance. I saw a tennis court to the left, a swimming pool to the right. There was even a driving range: four tees side by side on a little rise and yellow flags set up down the lawn in front to show you how far you'd hit the ball.

In the corner of the porch lay several rolls of tar paper, bundles of shingles, and a couple of toolboxes. Somebody had set up one of those long racks roofers use to cut and bend sheet metal.

Deputy Keen stopped at the glass door that let into the house from the porch.

"Here you go," he said.

The door had been broken in. It had been destroyed: glass all over the porch, all over the room inside, busted woodwork. Beside the door was a row of four concrete garden planters with some kind of ferns growing in them. The planters were maybe three feet high. Made of cement and full of dirt, the way they were, each one would have had to weigh well over a hundred pounds. Somebody had picked one of the planters up and thrown it through the porch door. He'd more than shattered the glass and the woodwork. He'd ripped the door and its upper hinge right out of the frame.

"Cat burglar, here, it looks like," I said.

Deputy Keen was looking at me. "That must have set off every house alarm in the state," he said.

"Man in a hurry," I said.

"Who do we know's in a hurry like that?"

"Here's your caretaker," I said.

A stout middle-aged man wearing a Red Sox cap came up onto the porch and joined us. I didn't know him.

"Buster Mayhew," said the man. He shook hands with me, nodded to the deputy. He looked at the ruined door and shook his head.

"Boy," he said.

"You want to go on in, see what's missing?" I asked him.

"What?"

"You want to take a look inside, see if anything's been stolen?"

"Oh," said Buster Mayhew. "Oh, sure. I guess so."

He stepped through the doorway into the house. The deputy and I followed.

The room we entered was a kind of living room. There was a fireplace in one wall, nice hardwood floor, big television, leather couches, low tables. Apart from the broken glass scattered over the floor, the planter lying in the glass, and the dirt and ferns that had spilled out of it, the room was clean and neat. Magazines and newspapers were arranged tidily on the tables. Deputy Keen had picked up a picture magazine and was looking at it. He put it down and picked up another. He showed it to me. On the cover was a photo of three plump young ladies standing in the snow in front of a grove of birch trees. They were wearing big square fur hats and nothing else — I mean nothing else. They were smiling and waving, the three of them there in the snow. They didn't look like they were a little cold, even. The titles above and below them were printed in Russian. In fact, all the papers and magazines were in Russian, with that strange alphabet they have that's so you have to look at it for a minute before you realize you can't even begin to read it.

"What are they, Russians?" Deputy Keen asked me.

"Looks like it," I said.

Deputy Keen turned to the caretaker. "Whose place is this?" he asked.

"Don't really know," said the caretaker. "They ain't here much."

"Who's here, when they are here?" I asked him.

"Foreigners," said the caretaker. "Some kind of foreigners. They don't speak no English. Germans? I don't know. I don't think so. I don't think they're Germans, but I don't know. They might be. I don't know nothing about them. I just look after the place, you know."

"Who do you work for?"

"Real estate company in Manchester."

"Which one?"

"O'Connor's."

"How long have you worked at this place?"

"God, I don't know. A year? Less? Less."

"Take a look around," I said. "Go ahead."

Buster Mayhew left us in the living room to go over the rest of the house. When we were alone, Deputy Keen turned to me again.

"You saw the roofers were here?" he asked.

"I saw their stuff."

"It didn't say which roofers, though, did it?"

"Not that I saw."

"I bet I know which ones, though, don't I?" said Deputy Keen.

"I don't know," I said. "Do you?"

"Timmy Russell, I bet. Who do you bet?"

"I'm not much of a betting man," I said.

Mayhew stood in the doorway. "They were in here," he said.

We left the living room and followed him to a smaller room set up as an office or study: a big desk, a chair behind it, other chairs, windows covered with heavy drapes. One wall was bookshelves, with books in Russian and a few in English. The desk drawers didn't lock. All of them had been pulled out and dumped onto the desk and onto the floor around it.

"Anything missing you can see?" Deputy Keen asked Mayhew.

"Oh, God, I don't know. I don't even know if I've been in this room before," said the caretaker. "I mostly look after the outside, you know."

"Roofers have been here, I guess," said Deputy Keen.

"That's right," said Mayhew. "They're reflashing the chimney. Been here since last week."

"Not here today, though," I said.

"No," said the caretaker. "They kind of come when they're ready, you know. It gets done."

"You gave them the gate code, then?" Keen asked him.

"Gate code?"

"For the security gate, down on the road. The electric gate?"

"Oh," said Mayhew. "Oh, sure. Sure, I did. Had to. I can't be here all the time waiting on them."

"You hire them?"

"That's right."

"Who'd you get?"

"Russell's crew," said the caretaker. "Out of Bellows Falls. You know them?"

"We know one of them," Deputy Keen said. Turning again to me, "Don't we?" he asked.

It looked like we'd done about all the damage we could do at the scene for the present, so the caretaker left to call his bosses at the management company and to get a sheet of plywood and whatever else he needed to secure the door. I gave him one of my sheriff cards to give to his company, so they could reach me.

I was on my way back to the office, but Deputy Keen stopped me as I was climbing into the truck.

"Sheriff?" he said.

I looked at him.

"Superboy works for Russell," said Keen. Superboy was what Keen and some others called Sean — young Sean Duke. It ain't what I called him. I called him Sean.

"He does," I said.

"He'd have the code for that gate," said Keen.

"He might," I said. "Might not."

"Superboy would break down that door, too. He'd do it just that way. That's pure Superboy. And plus, way out here, he'd know he could."

"Maybe."

"No maybe about it," said Keen. "An easy one, like I said."

"Like you said."

"I think I should go have a talk with Superboy," said Deputy Keen.

"I'll do that," I said.

"You will?"

"I'll talk to him," I said.

"No, you won't," said Deputy Keen.

"You don't think?"

"You mean like you talked to him about Van Horn's thing?"

"Van Horn's thing was nothing."

"Van Horn didn't think so, maybe."

"Sure, he did," I said. "Okay, Deputy. Thanks for your input. You go bust a speeder, now, why don't you?"

"Is that your order, here, Sheriff?"

"Sounds like it."

"I can see him on my own time," said the deputy.

"You can do whatever you like on your own time, Deputy."

The deputy gave me a dark look, nodded, and went to his patrol car. He drove off, leaving me alone at the house. I thought about going back inside and poking around some more, but why? All I'd find would be more of Sean's footprints. Everything Keen said was true. I knew that, he knew it, and he knew I knew it. That was the thing, right there. Because Deputy Keen and I don't exactly see eye to eye where Sean is concerned. No, we don't. And Deputy Keen is hard; Deputy Keen is stubborn. But Deputy Keen is not a fool. And Deputy Keen is ambitious.

So, no: I don't know Russian. But I know how to add. You see a little green fellow a foot and a half high with a couple of dozen eyes and antennas coming out of his head buying beer at the corner store on Wednesday. Ask him where he's in from, he says Mars. Then Saturday, here come a couple more of the same type fellows at the post office. How much more do you have to know to about decide the Martians are in town?

3

SHERIFFING

Now, I have said Deputy Keen and I don't think alike on the subject of young Sean Duke. That ain't the only place where we differ. For example, the deputy says this business in Grenada is an easy one. He says that because he knew right off who it was broke into the Russians' house, and he thinks if he knows who did the deed, and he takes them in, his job is done. But his job is sheriffing, and that ain't sheriffing. That's car repair. A car won't start, you say, Well, maybe the alternator's shot. You test it out. It don't work. You pull the old alternator, throw it away, put in a new one from the parts store, and you're done. Sheriffing's different. You can't do it with spare parts. It's a whole thing you're working on. It's a whole thing you have to keep going.

Truth is, Deputy Keen, Lyle, don't have much use for sheriffing. He reckons a sheriff is a kind of amateur cop. A soft cop. And that's so, in a way. The sheriff brings law to people who don't need law. He enforces the law for people who don't break it, or not much. Sheriffing is like being the bouncer at the Ladies' Aid lunch: when things are going normally, they don't work you too hard. Lyle's bored; he wants more. He's in a hurry.

Therefore he don't always see everything he needs to see. He don't always look both ways. That can lead to poor sheriffing. It can also lead to risk, because, again, sheriffing is enforcing the rules for people who nine times out of ten obey the rules on their own. But sheriffing don't necessarily go well on the tenth fellow. And it don't necessarily go well with people who don't know the rules, people from away.

Russians are from away, if anybody ever was.

But Lyle don't want to hear all that. He reckons he's a cut above sheriffing. Or, put it another way, he reckons he's a cut above sheriffing the way his boss does it, the way I do it. And Lyle's got an answer for that, too. Don't he just?

I learned sheriffing from old Ripley Wingate, who had the office here for about a hundred years. Wingate went in for a kind of horse-and-buggy sheriffing, and I was his deputy for ten or eleven years before he got done at seventy and I took over. Wingate could have had the job after seventy. He could have had the job after he'd died, at least for a while. Nobody was going to run against him, were they, any more than they're going to run against Diamond Mountain, or the moon, or anything else that's always been there.

That's another thing that sets sheriffing apart. Maybe that's the main thing: you're elected. You get voted in, and you get voted out. No other lawman is like that, that I ever heard of. The sheriff has to run for his job, every other year. Therefore you can't ever assume that you know even half as much as Deputy Keen thinks he knows about what that job is. And Lyle's only a deputy, don't forget. All he thinks he knows on sheriffing, and he ain't even the sheriff. Or he ain't, yet.

Not that Deputy Keen is a foreigner. He was born here in the county, in Humber, graduated from Cumberland Union. Basketball player. Lyle went to the Police Academy and took a job out of the county, with the police department in St. Johnsbury, looking to get into the state police. But the state police wouldn't have him. I don't know why. Lyle's a smart fellow, but, of course, with the state police smart won't do it for you. You have to have a genius IQ, or pretty close. Look at Trooper Timberlake.

Anyway, Lyle didn't take to it up in St. Johnsbury, so he applied to join our department, and I hired him. That's four or five years ago.

Again, Lyle's bright, and he's honest. He works hard. The occupational disease of sheriffing, you could say, is laziness, and Lyle don't have a lazy bone in him. Fact is, he might get too far over on the other side. Because Ripley Wingate used to tell us (me and his other deputies): Don't be lazy, but it's okay to look lazy. Lyle don't even look lazy. Far from it: his uniform's always pressed, his radio's always on his belt. He carries a gun.

I don't wear a uniform; no need of one. People around here know me. They know who I am. They know what I do. They don't have to see me in a fancy suit. I don't have a uniform, and I don't carry a weapon. Wingate never went armed. No guns, he said. Leave it in your car. And leave your car at home. I learned from Wingate. Of course, I have a gun. I have Wingate's old army .45 that he brought back from World War Two. It's in my sock drawer, where a gun ought to be. I also have the county's expensive Remington police shotgun in the trunk of the sheriff's car. At least I think it's in there. It was last time I looked. I don't much use the sheriff's car, though. I like my truck. Plus, it saves the county money.

Saving money is big. The sheriff is a county officer, but in this state the county don't have taxing authority; the towns do. Towns that don't have their own police forces — and that's practically all the little country towns — make a contract with the sheriff's department to take care of policing within their limits. Those town fees are what make the sheriff's budget. Therefore, the towns reckon that budget is their business — and that's fair enough. But, I mean, look at that Ambrose selectman the other day: those town boards and treasurers want to bite every dime you spend. They want to count your paper clips. They want to look over the tires on your patrol cars, and if they can see any tread at all on those tires, they want to know why you're asking for money to buy new ones.

You're a bookkeeper, is what it is. It don't ever end, and for time, it seems like it's two thirds of the job.

Wingate's right: you don't need a gun to be the sheriff. You don't need a badge or a uniform. You do need an adding machine.

I guess I could tell Lyle and my other deputies they're not to carry guns, the way Wingate told us years ago. I haven't done that. There are different kinds of people passing through here from what there used to be. Not long since, there was a sheriff's deputy up near White River who was shot and killed in a traffic stop. As near as anybody could tell, he'd pulled over a car for speeding or some other violation, went up to the car, and the driver shot him through the window and took off. Nobody ever found him. So I won't tell my deputies they can't arm themselves. Some of them do and some of them don't. I tell them to figure it out for themselves, do what they want. (Within reason: no nuclear weapons.) Again, Wingate didn't give them the choice, not in that, but Clemmie says I'm more Wingate than Wingate.

Clemmie's fond of Wingate. Wingate never married, he's all alone, and she feels sorry for him. After he'd retired we'd have him over for dinner now and then, or we'd take him out someplace, but not so much lately. He don't want it. He's by himself in his place over here in South Cardiff; it's just Wingate and his bees. He keeps bees.

He hasn't been well. Fact is, Wingate's barely making it. After all, he's eighty-three or -four. I go visit him every so often, but Clemmie don't come. Wingate don't want her. He don't want Clemmie to see him broken down the way he is, it looks like. If you're Wingate, you don't show weakness, or anyway you don't show it to women, or anyway you don't show it to women of an age to be your daughter. Wingate's old school.

4

THE SWEETHEART OF SIGMA CHI

Coming down the long drive from the Russians' house, I followed Deputy Keen. At the road, he went right and I went left. I wasn't going back to the department. I was going to look for Sean Duke. His parents lived in Afton. He wouldn't be at their place, but they might know where he was.

I had hoped Melrose wouldn't be home. I had hoped I'd be able to talk to Sean's mother. But Melrose was in front of their house when I drove up. He was washing his car, playing a garden hose over it to rinse off the soapsuds. He turned off the hose.

"Hello, Lucian," said Melrose. "You looking for Superboy?"

Melrose Tidd couldn't stand Sean. He wasn't Sean's real father. Sean's father had been dead for, at that time, I'd guess thirteen, fourteen years. Melrose was his stepfather.

"You know where I can find him?" I asked Melrose.

"Going to arrest him this time?" asked Melrose. "Going to take him in?"

"Nothing like that," I said.

"No," said Melrose, "I didn't think so. Not you, right? More likely you'd pat him on the head, ain't it? Get him to sit in your lap?"

"You know where I can find him?"

"Hell, no, I don't," said Melrose. "If you ain't going to bust him, then you can find him on your own."

Ellen came out of the house — Sean's mom. She'd seen us talking, and she came out drying her hands on a dish towel.

"Hello, Sheriff," said Ellen.

"He's after Superboy," said Melrose.

"Is that right?" Ellen asked me.

"I did want to talk to him."

"See?" said Melrose. "What'd he steal?"

"Shut up, Mel," said Ellen.

I talked to Ellen. "He's been working for Tim Russell's crew, hasn't he?" I asked her.

"For almost a year," said Ellen. "He's doing very well with it."

"That means he ain't in jail," said Melrose.

"Shut up, Mel," said Ellen.

"Yet," said Melrose.

Ellen shook her head at him.

"What do you want with him?" Melrose asked me.

"I want to talk to him," I said.

"Is he in trouble?" Ellen asked.

"Maybe," I said. "I don't know for sure. That's why I want to talk to him. You know where he is?"

"You mean today?" Ellen asked.

"Today would be good."

"Well," Ellen said. "If he's not at work, he'll be at Crystal's. She lives over in Monterey."

"She's got a trailer," Melrose said.

"Sean lives there, too," said Ellen.

"At night," said Melrose. "Some nights. When he ain't had a better offer."

"He and Crystal have been together since Christmastime," said Ellen.

"He got her in his stocking," said Melrose. "Along with the candy."

"Shut up, Mel," said Ellen.

————

The trailer where Sean lived with his girlfriend — his girlfriend, now — was one of half a dozen trailers on a lot back of the lumber-yard as you come into Monterey. It was an old trailer, a good deal older than either of the people living in it. Its siding was rusty, its windows were dirty, and it had a blue portable toilet set up off one corner.

I parked in front of the door and got out of the truck. There were no other vehicles at the trailer; there were no flowers or other plants in pots like any proper trailer ought to have. Only the little dirt yard, three cement blocks at the door for steps, and an off smell, faint but there alright, that must have come from the porta-ble. You can drive from the Russians' house, Disneyland, up on its own mountaintop, with its security gate, its tennis court, its pool, its golf range, its five-acre lawn — you can drive from there to this place in the same car, get there on the same day, in the same hour. It don't seem like you should be able to, but you can.

I knocked on the door. Right away a dog with a voice like a foghorn began barking inside. I stepped back from the door. The dog was roaring and banging against the door, making the door shake in its frame. Then a woman's voice started in yelling, "Jackson!" The dog shut up.

In a minute the trailer's door opened, and a young woman stood in the doorway. No sign of the dog, no sound.

"What is it?" the girl asked.

"I'm Sheriff Wing," I said.

"I know who you are. What do you want?"

The girl looked like she'd just woke up. She was about twenty; she had a lot of curly red hair. Her legs and feet were bare. Her toenails were painted blue. She had a tattoo going around the upper part of her right arm, a snake, like a purple snake winding around her bare arm there. Nasty looking thing. She wore a T-shirt that came down just far enough to make her decent. Decent — speaking legally.

"Sean here?" I asked her.

"No."

"Do you know where he is?"

"Working."

"Are you Crystal?"

"I don't have to tell you that," said the girl. "I don't have to tell you who I am. I don't have to tell you nothing."

The girl's T-shirt had SHIT HAPPENS printed over its front; the letters were pushed out in front of her chest. She was a well-put-together girl, no question. Now she raised the shirt and took a cigarette from a pack she had tucked in the elastic of her black underpants. She lit the cigarette and leaned in the door frame, looking at me in the yard.

"What's your last name?" I asked her.

"I don't have to tell you that, either," said the girl. "Here's the thing. Why don't you fuck off?" She blew cigarette smoke into the yard, then bent at the waist to scratch her ankle. We had Jeannie with the Light Brown Hair, here, it looked like. We had the Sweetheart of Sigma Chi.

"Sean is working at a big fancy place in Grenada," I said. "I need to see him about that place. Will he be here later?"

Right then, for some reason, her dog started in barking again. By its bark, it was a good, big dog. The Sweetheart of Sigma Chi turned in her doorway.

"Jackson!" she shouted. "Shut the fuck up!"

The dog stopped barking.

"Is Sean coming by here later?" I asked again.

"Ask him. I don't have to tell you that. I don't have to talk to you at all. Leave us alone."

I got out one of my sheriff cards and handed it to the girl. She took it and held it, but she didn't look at it.

"Tell Sean to give me a call when he gets in," I said. "Will you do that?"

"If I say yes, will you fuck off?" the girl asked me.

"Sure."

"Okay, then," said the girl. "I'll tell him." She stepped back into the trailer and slammed the door, and I climbed into the truck and started for home.

The girl was a Cumberland girl. I knew her, but I couldn't remember her last name right off. She waitressed at a hamburger place on the way to Brattleboro. She'd gone to school down there, too, not to Cumberland Union, where by rights she should have gone. It seemed like she didn't get on with her father, or her mother, or something along those lines. Hard to believe.

Finn, her name was, the Sweetheart of Sigma Chi. Crystal Finn. Now she was going with Sean. They all did, sooner or later, it looked like, all the girls. This was her turn. Sean got around. He was good looking, I guess: he was big and strong, and he had that kind of bold grin that makes some women think, Well, this fellow's pretty sure of himself. He's pretty confident. He must have something. He obviously don't have it in his brains. Maybe he's got it in his shorts. Let's find out.

Yes, Sean was quite the stud horse. He'd had the pants off half the women in the county. You had to wonder how he did it. Well, not how he did it, but how he was able to stand the strain. I couldn't, I know that. 'Course, I never had to. The first and only girl who ever took a second look at me, I married.

Sean's father, Dougie Duke, grew up in Mount Pleasant. Shortstop. He'd gone right into the service after school, and they'd shipped him out to the Persian Gulf, as part of the first show over there. Two boys from the county had gone: Dougie and one of the Lawrences from Cardiff Center. I don't know where that Lawrence is today, but Dougie's right here. He got blown up, blown all to pieces, and he came home in a bag with a whole bus full of soldiers in full dress to give him a military burial here in the west cemetery in Fayetteville.

Well, pretty much the whole town turned out for that, with the family sitting on folding chairs from the fire house and everybody else standing among the gravestones. It was pretty rough, too. Dougie's father couldn't even bring himself to go. His mom and Ellen, his wife, and their two girls were in bad shape in the front, crying and weeping. So were a lot of other people.

But the boy, Sean — he'd have been five, six — was off a little to one side by himself, standing all alone. A skinny, scrawny little kid then, before he got his growth. Somebody had dressed him up in a blue suit jacket and a tie. The jacket was too big, it hung on him like a tent, and the tie came down most of the way to his knees. His mother tried to get him to come sit by her, but he wouldn't. He'd moved away from her and stood by himself, a little apart, just stood there, perfectly still, not looking to the right or to the left but staring at the ground in front of him, bewildered, looking like the last little boy on earth. He had no idea what was going on. He'd just stand there as still as he could and not look at anything or anybody, and wait till it was over.

When the honor guard had fired its rifles and folded the flag and handed it to Ellen, Clemmie lost it. We were standing with the others, and she was crying, and she turned to me and nodding toward Sean where he stood alone, she whispered to me, "Why doesn't he cry?"

"He don't know how," I told Clemmie. But my voice wasn't right either, somehow, it seemed like, so I cleared my throat and said again, "He don't know how."

Always, then, Sean was the kid who'd lost his father, and people didn't forget that. Sean carried a kind of permanent credit balance in that account. Sure, he did. Though why, exactly? Yes, this is a small place, but we're in the same fix here as anywhere else: too many kids, too few parents — in particular, too few fathers. And if Sean was different because his old man hadn't walked out or been thrown out but had been killed in a war, well, he wasn't by himself there, either, was he? Come to that, I'm in the same spot myself: my father was killed in 1943 in one of the big aircraft carrier battles in the Pacific. I never knew him, never saw him. He never saw me. If you get a free pass for criminal behavior along with your dad's GI death benefit, then why ain't I a housebreaker, like Sean, or a bank robber, or a congressman?

Not that Sean got extra slack from everyone: his stepfather, Melrose, hated his guts, and Sean got up Deputy Keen's nose in the worst way. He got up Keen's nose like a little fire ant. Keen had been trying to hang Sean for a couple of years, but he couldn't close the deal. For that he blamed me. There was Mr. Van Horn, for example.

Stanton Van Horn had a summer place in Gilead. He was a rich fellow, the kind of fellow collects sports cars. One night a couple of years ago somebody hot-wired one of Mr. Van Horn's cute little Porsches and took it for a ride before crashing it into a tree on the South Cardiff road and leaving it there with the floorboards all over empty Genesee cans. Sean turns up the next day with a bad hangover and a bump on his head, says he was overserved at a party in Brattleboro and walked into a door. A lot of people didn't believe him. One of them was Lyle Keen. Another was me, but I didn't see going to war over the business. Was I supposed to bring in the crime lab team for, what, a joyride? Van Horn hadn't even known his Porsche was missing until Beverly called him.

Of course, we had to do a report. Deputy Keen wrote it up, copy to Van Horn for his insurance company. I filed the original, had a quiet chat with Van Horn. Van Horn's happy. He buys himself another Porsche. I told Deputy Keen to stand down.

The deputy didn't like that. No, he did not. He don't forget it, either, and he don't let me forget it. He reckons I'm letting young Sean run the gate. He ain't the only one thinks that, either. Well, maybe they're right. Maybe I am. But it looks to me like when Wingate's gone, about all we'll have left around here will be Deputy Keen and Trooper Timberlake and the like of them. All we'll have left will be the Eagle Scouts. All the old-timers will be gone except for me, and — in a kind of a way, except for Sean himself.

— 5 —

IT IS WHAT IT IS

How do people get to be where they are? I don't mean in any fancy way, but just that: where they are at. Location, location, location is what counts, they tell you, and they're right. Where have you passed through to get here, what's your geography? It looks as though you can work it either of two ways: straight line or winding. Some people, if they left tracks all through their lives and you could follow them, you'd find they wandered around like a deer in the snow. They see an ad in the paper, and the next thing they know, they're in California. They meet a fellow in a bar, and they take off for Texas. They get in a card game, and in another week they find themselves in New York City. If you ask them how they wound up here, and not someplace else, they'd need a — what is a book of maps, a big book, to tell you? — they'd need an atlas. With those people, getting to where they are has a lot of luck to it, it looks like. Luck, or call it chance.

They're not me, those people. I'm the other way: straight line. It's like I was born at the station, got right aboard the train, and then went along on the rails. Started here, here I am, here I'll finish up. Clemmie's and my house today in Fayetteville village is just four houses down from the house where I grew up. Four houses down and across the road. You don't get much straighter a line than that, do you?

Though with me, too, I guess, some part of geography was up to chance. I didn't have to go the road I did. I wasn't locked in. Every day there was another turn I could have taken; there were a thousand other turns. But I didn't. Others did, but not me. Am I sorry about that? Maybe, a little, sometimes. Not much. This is my life, it looks like, this one here. One to a customer is the rule. It is what it is.

Born at the station? Well, not quite, but near it. Our backyard went down to the old narrow-gauge right-of-way. I could have walked out our kitchen door and flagged the train — except that the train quit running long before I was born. The trains were gone; the tracks were gone. The railroad had become a kind of fading path in the woods. But there was the old depot in the village. It held Arthur Tavistock's collection of dead tractors, but it had been the train depot. That was the station where I was, so to speak, born.

I went to the old academy in Cardiff. I liked it, stayed out of trouble, was a pretty good third baseman. Not much of a scholar, though I took the college prep course. And there's chance, right there, too, because I wanted to take auto mechanics, but my mother wouldn't hear of it. School was school, she said, a garage was a garage. So I prepared for no-college. But for that, I might be fixing cars in China today rather than being a highly uneducated lawman right here in the valley.

Got out of school and joined the navy, the same as my father (though I lived to tell the tale and he didn't) — one more in the long line of blue-water men to come out of New England's only landlocked state. You'll see the world, the navy tells you, and you do, in a manner of speaking. You see your ship, miles and miles and weeks and weeks of gray steel, and you see a whole world of places you never want to see again.

Though it's true I didn't see a lot of shipping. I found what so many sailors before me have: I don't much care for ships. I did my tour in the shore patrol, the navy's police force. So I was on dry land, first at Long Beach, then Da Nang. In the shore patrol I found out that I have a talent for talking to people who are very, very drunk. And I learned that if talking don't work, you can do about anything you like with a drunk by grabbing tight hold of his nose and twisting. You won't do permanent damage, but he will come along, plus he'll put out quite a lot of blood, which changes the subject, makes him think, and impresses any friends of his who might want to join in the fun. Busting drunks and breaking up fights. That's what I did in the navy.

Got home in spring '69. I might have never been away, except for no more school. What to do? Well, my uncle Stuart was a logger, he could always use a new hand who, being family, he wouldn't have to pay very well. I joined his crew, and for a year I worked in the woods. But logging's more dangerous than anything I did or saw anybody else doing in Vietnam. A year of it was enough for me.

I thought about going back to school, but what for? There was nothing I wanted to do that more school would make me better at. I drove truck for a doughnut distributor, but that ain't a real job. I quit. Was I restless? You could say I was restless.

Then somebody told me the state police would like my having been shore patrol. I put in my application, and they did. They did like that. They took me on.

So, a year and change with the Green and Gold. I liked the work, but I can't say I ever liked the state police. No fault of theirs; they're a military organization, basically, they have to be, and I thought I'd had about enough of military organizations in the navy. Plus, I was going out with Clemmie by then, and she plain refused to marry anybody who might be seen wearing one of those flat-brimmed cowboy hats the troopers have.

Yes, I married above myself; everybody says so. Clemmie says so. Her old friends say so. Her cousins say so. Her father don't say so. He don't have to.

Not that we were ever poor in our family. We were never poor, not close. My sisters and I could have anything we wanted. We had a deal with our mother. Her end was, we could have anything we wanted. Our end was, we wouldn't want too much.

That was the same deal everybody's family had. Well, not Clemmie's, maybe. Her father did alright. He did better than alright. He still does. Addison's an attorney. He's not a local, exactly, though he's not far off. He grew up in Brattleboro; his father was a doctor down there. His grandfather was governor of the state, or maybe it was his great-grandfather. Addison went to law school in Philadelphia, then came back to set up as a lawyer, not in Brattleboro, but here up the valley, in Fayetteville. He has his office right around back of the courthouse.

Addison's a funny fellow in some ways. He's no woodchuck, he's a graduate of Harvard, and he's traveled. He's lived in England, France, Italy — places like that. But he wants you to believe he's just a country lawyer, sitting around the store playing checkers with the farmers and spitting on the stove. And, in a way, that's what he is — and, in a way, it ain't.

For example, when the state condemned Oscar Breedlove's gas station over here in Dead River Settlement because his underground tanks had been leaking for years, and Oscar decided to sue the Exxon Corporation, whose gas he'd sold and whose contractor put in the tanks, who showed up in court representing Exxon? Addison does a good deal of that kind of work for out-of-state interests, I guess. Maybe you can't get rich lawyering for people here in the county, but lawyering for Exxon might be a different thing.

Clemmie's an only child. There's a certain weight to that, she'll tell you, and it looks like she's got it double, since her mother don't live here. She and Addison split up when Clemmie was little. In those days, in a place like this, being divorced pretty much made Clemmie's mom a fallen woman. She would have found it hard to stay around here if she'd wanted to. As it was, though, she had other plans. Clemmie's mom was a New Yorker, and she moved back down there. She remarried, had a couple more kids. Clemmie don't see much of her.

Addison stayed single. He and Clemmie lived in their house here on the Devon road, though Clemmie spent a good deal of time in Brattleboro, being partly raised by her aunt and uncle, Addison's sister and her husband down there.

So Addison has been a bachelor for years. He's had lady friends from time to time, and that's had to have been a little tough on Clemmie, a little confusing, when she was a girl, anyway, especially because some of Addison's lady friends have been married to other people. Nobody makes a fuss, though. People are going to do what they're going to do. Addison's what you could call a pillar of the community, though he's the kind of pillar where the side facing out gets a little more paint than the side facing in. He likes his toddy, too. And he's getting older. Like Clemmie says, a certain weight.

Give him credit, though, Addison. He's honest. He don't lie, he don't sneak. The time I stopped him for driving under the influence, I had him pulled over, and he started to get out of his car and about fell on his face.

"Have you had anything to drink, sir?" I asked him

"Don't insult both our integillences, Trooper," said Addison. "What did I say? Did I say 'integillences'? I believe I did. I must be intoxicated. *Intelligences*. Don't insult our *intelligences*, Trooper. Do your duty." And he handed over his keys. That was pure Addison.

Addison didn't think much of the idea of his only daughter marrying a policeman. He for sure didn't think much of it when Clemmie and I were getting engaged and I quit the state police to be a sheriff's deputy. If you have to have a cop for a son-in-law, at least let him be a high-class cop and not some shitkicker. Poor Addison.

———

No, going from the state police to the sheriff's department didn't make sense. When I told my barracks commander what I was doing, "God damn it," he said, "you're playing in Fenway, here, and you want to quit and go to Pawtucket?" He was a good man, though. "Well," he went on, "you could do worse. You'll be with Ripley Wingate, up there. You could do a lot worse. Give him my regards. Tell him he's getting my best boy, god damn him. It ain't true, but tell him anyway."

A good man. But what about Wingate? Where did he come from? I knew I wasn't cut out for the state police, but I didn't know I wanted to go to the sheriff's. I didn't know, but Wingate did.

There are no strangers in law enforcement: everybody knows everybody else, at least some. And, of course, Wingate had been sheriff it seemed like all my life. So sure, I knew him, at least by sight. But Wingate and I hadn't spoken ten words before this time. Then one day when I'd been in the troopers for a year and a bit, I was patrolling in North Cameron on the Ulster road. It was a spring day. I had the windows open. I came around a bend, and here's Wingate's sheriff's car pulled over in a turnout, and Wingate himself standing beside it and looking my way.

I thought maybe he was having engine trouble, so I drove in beside him and stopped.

"Good morning, Sheriff," I said.

"Trooper Wing," said Wingate.

"Is everything okay?"

"Pretty day like this? 'Course it is."

"What are you doing up here?" I asked him.

"Waiting for you," said Wingate. "Get on out and stand with me a minute, why don't you? Take in the air."

I left my patrol car, and Wingate and I leaned on his car and looked out in front of us across the road and over a big mowing beyond it going up to the top of a hill. There was an old house up there, an old farmhouse and a barn, and the clouds moving behind them in the blue sky.

"You're Lucian, right?" Wingate asked me.

"That's right, Sheriff," I said.

"What do they call you, then?"

"Lucian."

Wingate nodded. " 'Course they do," he said. "Well, here's the thing, Lucian. You've been at the barracks now for, what, a couple of years?"

"Not that long. Year and a half."

"A year and a half. And yet, you know, I've been noticing something about you."

"What's that, Sheriff?"

"How'm I to put it?" said Wingate. "Let's see: you were in the service, weren't you?"

"Three years in the navy."

"The navy," said Wingate. "I was army, but it's the same: your officers, when they dress up, they wear swords, don't they? For ceremonial occasions? Naval officers?"

"I guess so. Some of them. Sometimes."

"And you've seen them," Wingate went on, "wearing their swords?"

"I guess I have."

"Then you've seen how a man walks, you've seen how he carries himself when he's wearing a sword," Wingate went on. "Kind of stiff and ramrod, and favoring one side so the sword don't trip him up?"

"Uh-huh."

"Well, it always struck me that when young fellows like yourself go into the barracks, there, the state police, that when they've been there a little while, they always, all of them, start walking like they're wearing a sword. Have you seen that?"

"I can't say I have, Sheriff."

"I have," said Wingate. "I bet they do, too. I bet they do so give them swords. Don't they? At the barracks? They do so wear swords. At night, maybe, when nobody's around?"

"I wouldn't know, Sheriff," I said. "I never did."

"You never did," said Wingate. "That's it. That's what I noticed. You're different. You've been there near two years, and you haven't started, you haven't developed that walk. That sword walk. Which makes me wonder: are you happy in your work, Trooper Wing?"

"I don't know."

"Yes, you do," said Wingate. "If that's your answer, you do know. You know you ain't. Now, here's the thing. I'm hiring a deputy this spring. Deputy Rackstraw's getting done. He's got a security job at the power plant. I need to hire another deputy. I wondered if that's anything that might interest you."

"That would be a pay cut, I guess," I said.

"You guess right," said Wingate. "It would be a pay cut. It would be a hell of a pay cut. I ain't got the governor behind me, you know."

"Well," I said, "I'm getting married in the summer, though."

"That don't matter," said Wingate. "You're supposed to be poor when you're just married, ain't you?"

"I don't know," I said.

"Who are you marrying?" Wingate asked me.

"Clemmie Jessup."

"Addison's girl?"

"That's right, Sheriff."

"What are you worried about, then?" asked Wingate. "You'll get by. Have Addison set you up."

"No chance, Sheriff," I said.

"No chance because Addison won't do it, or no chance because you won't let him?"

"Both, it looks like."

"Well, but still, think it over," said Wingate. "You ain't got to make up your mind now."

"I will. I will think it over."

"Sure," said Wingate. "You think it over. Think it over good. The sheriff ain't the barracks, you know. It's like, it's like the difference between going fishing with a cane pole and taking off all your clothes and jumping into the pond and swimming around with the fish all day and maybe grabbing one from time to time."

"Which is which, Sheriff?"

"Sheriff's swimming around with the fish," said Wingate.

"I'll get back to you," I said.

"It's like the difference between being the fellow who puts the doors and windows in a big house and being the fellow who builds a little house, but he builds the whole thing," said Wingate.

"I'll think it over."

"Sheriff's the one builds the whole house," said Wingate.

"I thought so," I said.

"There ain't a sword in the shop," said Wingate.

I was on patrol that morning, supposed to be, so I left Wingate, promising to think about his deputy job. I thought about it for two minutes. No, I didn't. I didn't think about it that long. I didn't think about it at all; I didn't have to.

The next day I turned in my flat hat.

DARK LADY

Wednesday we had the day off. Not a Russian to be seen, not a Russian heard from. No Russians on the market anywhere. I'd about decided I'd have to get busy and scare one up. Then, Thursday, bright and early, the Russians began to come to me.

The sheriff's department has its headquarters in Fayetteville, across the common from the county courthouse. Wingate, in his time, had a little broom closet of an office in the courthouse basement, but since then we've moved on, though not real far. I could walk to work if I wanted to, but then where would I be if I had to saddle up in a hurry and ride out after evildoers? I take the truck, as a rule, and I like to get in to the department first thing, before the night dispatch goes home, so I can talk to a human being about what I don't know happened the night before instead of reading a log or listening to a recording. That works when the night dispatch is sharp, like Beverly is during the day, or even halfway sharp, but at night the sharp kind is hard to find. I always wondered why. Night dispatch at our department is a quiet job: good job for a reader, good job for a crossword puzzle man, good job for a knitter. You don't have to be a deputy. You'd think plenty of people would want a job like that. But no, the night dispatch turns over pretty quick.

The one we had now was new, Errol Toobin. Errol was middle-aged, didn't have much to say. Kind of a low-gear fellow who had worked in a hardware store for years until his bad back made him quit because he couldn't stand up all day anymore. He had some disability pension, and he'd been looking for a job where he could sit down. I'd just let go the fellow we'd had for dispatching under the influence of alcohol. (Night dispatch is also a good job for a drinker.) So Errol had started at the department. He'd figured out how to turn the radio on and off, and we were working on the rest.

Wednesday-Thursday night hadn't stretched Errol too far, it didn't look like. Somebody had rolled his car on Route 10, and there was a noise complaint from Mount Pleasant. That was the sum of it. Errol was getting ready to go home. I started for my office in the rear.

"Oh," said Errol. "Forgot: somebody in there to see you."

"In here?"

"She's been waiting for a couple of hours," said Errol.

"She?"

"Didn't say her name. She wanted to see you. I told her to wait in there."

"Next time," I said, "somebody comes in, you're by yourself, put them out front, here, where you can see them."

"Why?" Errol asked.

"So we don't have people wandering all over the office," I said.

"Roger that," said Errol.

"Just ask them to have a seat out here," I said. "Maybe get them a cup of coffee."

"Roger that," said Errol

"It's a matter of security, you might say," I told him.

"Roger that," said Errol. He was coming along, no question.

I opened the door to my office and looked in. A woman stood up from the chair I kept in front of the desk and turned to face me.

"Sheriff Wing?" she asked.

She was nobody I knew from the county, nobody I had ever seen before. Tall, tall as I am, slim, somewhere in her middle thirties, dark brown hair worn long. She didn't look like she spent a lot of time in police stations, but she also didn't look like she couldn't handle herself in one. She didn't look like there were many places where she couldn't handle herself.

"I'm Wing," I said. I went around to my desk, and we both sat, the desk between us.

The woman bent and picked a paper shopping bag off the floor beside her chair. She set it on the desk. "From Sean," she said.

"Sean?"

"Sean Duke," said the woman. "He said you knew him."

"I know him," I said. "I don't know you."

"I'm Morgan Endor," the woman said.

"Morgan?"

"Morgan Endor."

"Morgan's your first name?"

"That's right, Sheriff. It's a family name. Sean asked me to bring you these."

She didn't empty the bag out onto the desk. Instead, she stood up and, reaching into the bag, began pulling things out of it and laying them neatly in a pile in front of me. I watched her.

A sport jacket, a pair of jeans, a white shirt, a man's undershirt, underpants, two socks, a wristwatch, a billfold. I took the billfold. In it was a card from a Super 8 Motel in Montreal and a California driver's license issued to Oswaldo de Gomez, Los Angeles. No money. I set the billfold to one side.

I looked up at Morgan Endor. Morgan. What kind of a name is that for a woman? She had stopped taking things from the bag. She was watching me.

"Where did Sean get this?" I asked her.

"Wait," she said.

She reached back into the bag and carefully, holding it by the butt, she took out a small pistol and laid it on top of the pile of clothes. It was one of those imported semiautomatics, clever little things that look like you're meant to take them with you to the opera.

"Is it loaded?" she asked me.

I picked up the pistol, dropped the magazine out of the butt, and drew back the slide. The round in the chamber popped out and landed on the desk, where it rolled toward the woman. She put out her finger and stopped it. I laid the gun back down on top of the pile of clothes.

"Not now," I said.

Morgan Endor pushed the cartridge across the desk to me. I took it and put it in a drawer.

"Is that all?" I asked.

She went into the bag for the last time and came up with a piece of paper, folded, which she handed to me. Then she sat down again in the chair.

"That's for you from Sean," she said.

I didn't open the paper or handle the other things. I picked up the billfold again and took out the driver's license. It was a photo license. I had another look at the picture.

"Where did you say Sean came by these?" I asked.

"He took them away from the person who had them. Read the note."

I unfolded the paper. It read like this:

SHERF LUCAN
I BUSTED UP THAT FUKING SPIC + LEFT HIM WERE
EVEN YOU CUD FIND. HA. ALSO TOOK HIS CLOSE +

WALET HER THEY ARE. ALSO HIS PECE YOU CAN AD
IT TO YOUR COLECTON. HA. DON'T SEND NO MORE
FUKING SPICS FORINERS
RESPETFULY
S. DUKE
P.S. HIS WALLETT HAD $500. YOU CAN PUT IT ON
MY TAB.
HA.

I put the note down on the desk and leaned back in my chair.
"You're a friend of Sean's?" I asked.

"An acquaintance."

"How?"

"How what, Sheriff?"

"How do you know him?"

"He's been working at my house."

"Where's your house?"

"Mount Zion. It's my parents' house, actually. I've been staying
there this spring and summer."

"What was Sean doing there?"

"He was fixing the roof," said Morgan Endor. "The roof started
to leak. I told my father. He called somebody. They sent Sean."

"You live there with your parents?"

"No. They live in Provence."

"Provence?"

"It's part of France, Sheriff."

"Is that right?"

"Yes. I'm living at their house here temporarily so I can get some
work done."

"You got to know Sean when he was working on your roof?"

"Yes. I watched him. We talked. I saw I could use Sean."

"Use him?"

"In my work."

"What kind of work is that?"

"Photography."

"You're a photographer?"

"Yes."

"And Sean helped you take pictures?"

"Not exactly. I wanted to photograph him."

"Photograph Sean?"

"That's right."

"Why?"

"Sean is beautiful."

That brought me up some, I have to say. I probably could have thought of a better way of asking the next few questions.

"What do you take pictures of, Ms. Endor?"

"Men."

"Men?" I asked her. "You mean, like me?"

"Not like you. Young men."

"Young men. What kind of pictures are we talking about, here?"

She lifted her chin an inch and gave me a look.

"How extraordinary," she said. "You think I'm a pornographer, don't you, Sheriff?"

"I wouldn't know," I said. "I don't know any pornographers."

"I do," said Morgan Endor. "But I'm not one of them. I'm an artist. I'm preparing for a show in the fall, actually. That's why I'm here."

"A photography show?"

"Yes. They're not uncommon, believe it or not."

"Where's the show?"

"Paris."

"I'll bet that's Paris, France, ain't it?"

"That's right, Sheriff."

"That anywhere near Provence?"

"Not near, not far."

"What kind of show?"

"The show is about style," said Morgan Endor. "Or say it's about personality. Personal style."

"You're saying Sean has style?"

"No. Sean is without style. That's his power. What Sean has is an interior."

"An interior?"

"An inner life. Sean has a great vulnerability, a great delicacy."

"You can tell that from his note," I said.

Morgan Endor didn't say anything, but she kept that look steady, leveled right between my eyes.

"Okay, Ms. Endor," I said after a minute. "Maybe you're right about Sean. But I ain't concerned about his inner life. I think he might be in trouble. I need to talk to him. Where is he?"

"He was at my house from about midnight," she said. "He had these things with him. He'd been in some kind of fight with whoever had them, I gather. He asked me to take them to you, with the note. I did."

"You left him there?" I asked. "He's still at your place?"

"No. He left, too."

"To go where?"

"He didn't say."

"You said he'd been in a fight. Was he hurt?"

"Not that I saw. He was keyed up. This other man had actually come after Sean, I gather, and Sean had, I gather, beaten him in self-defense and taken his clothes. Sean's very physical."

"Uh-huh."

"I was interested in that about him, as well," said Morgan Endor.

"I bet," I said.

No answer, but she cocked the hammer on the look she'd been giving me.

"Did Sean say anything about the fellow he'd had the fight with?" I asked. "The fellow whose things we've got?"

"He was after him," she said. "That's all. Sean said the man had followed him, was after him."

"He say why?"

"No."

I handed her the license. "You know him?" I asked.

"No."

"Never seen him anyplace?"

"No." She looked closer at the photo. "Gomez?" she said. "He doesn't look like a Latin type, does he?"

"He sure don't," I said.

She left a little after that. I gave her one of my sheriff cards and asked her to get Sean to come see me. She said she would. I wasn't holding my breath for it, though. Morgan Endor made two women Sean had put up between me and him (three if you counted his mom). I wondered if this last one knew about the Sweetheart of Sigma Chi, with her blue toenails and her snake tattoo and her SHIT HAPPENS T-shirt, back there in her trailer — her and Sean's trailer. I would have guessed no, but you can't ever tell with a fellow like Sean, who's got a inner life.

————

Morgan Endor had just gone when Deputy Keen came into my office. He looked at the pile of clothes with the little pistol on top.

"What's this?" he asked.

"From Sean," I said. I showed him the license.

"Seen him around?" I asked Lyle.

"Nope," he said. "Gomez? California? What is he, a Mexican? He don't look like a Mexican, does he?"

"He ain't," I said. "He's a Russian. He's the fellow Timberlake had up on Diamond the other night."

"The nude?"

"Same fellow," I said.

"What makes you think so?"

"What makes me think so? I was there. I saw him. We had to wrestle the fellow to get him into the ambulance. It's him. He was talking Russian."

"How come he's got a California license?" Lyle asked.

"Paid for it, I would guess," I said. "Get one for you, too, you want one. Get you a couple. How many you need?"

"What are you going to do?"

"Well," I said. "Call the barracks, to start with. Timberlake and them took the fellow down there the other night. Maybe they've still got him."

"I doubt it," said Lyle.

"Me, too," I said.

I picked up the phone to call the state police barracks in Brattleboro. Then I put it down again.

"Tell you what," I said to Deputy Keen. "You're so hot to work on this case? Why don't you take a ride out to Monterey, see Sean's girlfriend out there. Crystal. You know Crystal?"

"Don't know the lady," said Lyle. "I thought you'd talked to her."

"We didn't hit it off too good," I said. "See her. See if you can get anywhere with her, get any kind of line on where Sean has got to."

"I can do that," said Lyle. "What if he's there, Superboy? What if he's with her? Bust him?"

"No. Walk away. Call in."

"Walk away? The hell I will."

"The hell you won't. Unless you want to lose your badge."

The deputy turned and started out of the office.

"Deputy?"

He stopped. "Sheriff?" he said, not turning, keeping his back to me.

"If she does, if she gives you any line on Sean, I don't want you galloping off after him. You call in. That clear?"

"That's clear, Sheriff."

Deputy Keen left the office on a head of steam so hot you could hear him whistle. Another contented employee.

When the deputy had gone, I called Brattleboro. I asked to talk to Lieutenant Farabaugh, the chief investigator down there. Dwight Farabaugh had started with the state police the same time I had, but he'd stuck with it. In his time, to put it the way Wingate did, Dwight had carried as big a sword as any, but he was getting ready to retire now. He'd been in the barracks a long time, he knew me, and sometimes he'd talk to me in English.

"Well, Lucian," Dwight came on the line. "How are things up in the woods? Pretty quiet?"

"Pretty," I said. "Had some excitement, though. You must have heard about it. Foreign fellow in a profound state of undress, became unruly, kind of, with your Trooper Timberlake. He ended up down there, as a matter of fact."

"Oh," said Dwight, "you're talking about Ivan the Terrible."

"I probably am," I said. "Where's he?"

"Oh, he's long gone," said Dwight. "Ivan was the star of the show around here for a little while. But, you know how it is, Lucian. Somebody held up a Seven-Eleven on Route 10, and now Ivan's old news. How quick we forget."

"Ain't that the truth?" I said. "Did you ever figure out who he was, though?"

"Oh, sure, we did," said Dwight. "Hang on."

I heard him rattle some papers. Then he came back on the line.

"Let's see," said Dwight. "Yevgeny Karagin. Yevgeny. That's the same name as Eugene. Did you know that?"

"I didn't."

"Born Moscow, USSR, 1975. Current citizenship, Czech. First arrested, Moscow, 1993. Arrested Vienna, Austria, 1996; again 1998. Grand theft. Arrested Rome, Italy, 2000. Arrested Mexico City, 2002. Fellow's practically the whole damn UN, ain't he? Decided to try his luck in the land of opportunity, it looks like. Arrested Dallas, 2002. Narcotics trafficking. Made bail. Took off. Can you believe it? The man jumped his bail. He absconded. Who'd have predicted that, Lucian? I'll bet that surprised the hell out of them down in Dallas. Be that as it may, Ivan's now a federal fugitive. Came in here last winter from Montreal on a US passport issued to Oswaldo de Gomez of Los Angeles."

"You ran his prints for all that?"

"We did," said Dwight. "Didn't have much else to run, did we, seeing the condition of total, extreme buck nakedness in which the subject was received from your jurisdiction. Ran his prints. Got a hit via FBI. From Interpol. Get that, Lucian? Interpol. Pretty fancy stuff."

"What happened to him?"

"Ivan? Oh, we kicked him right up to Immigration on the border. Fired him right up there, I can tell you. We want nothing to do with fellows like Ivan. You know that. By now he's on his way back to Moscow."

"Okay. I'm much obliged to you, Lieutenant."

"What have you got going up there that brings in this kind of critter, Lucian?"

"I ain't got nothing going," I said. "I got to wondering about him, is all. Like you said, it's quiet up here."

"Sure, it is. Sure, you did," said Dwight. "Is there anything else you need me to tell you, Lucian?"

"I don't guess so, Lieutenant," I said.

"Is there anything I need you to tell me?"

"I don't guess so, Lieutenant."

"Alright, then."

———

Clemmie looked at me over the top of the magazine she was reading. "Sean?" she said. "Why do you ask?"

"This photographer lady thinks he's beautiful," I told her. "'Sean's beautiful,' she said. You think Sean's beautiful?"

"Sean?" said Clemmie. "No. I don't know. No. He's . . . I don't know. He's kind of cute, I guess. He's got a nice mouth."

"A nice mouth?"

"Well, yes," said Clemmie. "Or, no. I don't know. Why ask me? What's Sean done now?"

"I think he broke into a vacation place up in Grenada," I said. "I don't know that, but I think he did. Lyle Keen sure thinks he did. Then he — Sean — had a run-in with some fellow who nobody can figure out but who might be connected to the house Sean broke into."

"A run-in?" asked Clemmie. "You mean a fight?"

"Call it that, I guess," I said. "Kind of one-sided, maybe. Call it half a fight."

"Was he hurt?"

"Not too bad. A little knocked around. Might have had his shoulder dislocated, it looked like. Hard to say; he couldn't speak English."

"Who couldn't?"

"The fellow. Russian fellow, he was."

"No," said Clemmie. "Not him. Sean. I meant Sean. Was Sean hurt?"

"Oh. No. Not Sean. Sean knows how to fight."

"He does?"

"If he don't, he should. He's done enough of it, here and there."

"I always think of him at the funeral," said Clemmie. "That sad, sad little boy."

"He ain't a little boy any more."

"No," said Clemmie. "He isn't. You said a photographic lady. What photographic lady?"

"Lady up in Mount Zion," I said. "She's a photographer. She takes photos. Takes photos of men. Get it? She thinks Sean's beautiful. He's her model, or something, it looks like."

"What does that mean, her model?"

"What do you think it means?" I said. "I asked you, though: is she right? Is Sean beautiful?"

"I couldn't tell you," said Clemmie. "He's not my type."

— 7 —

THE ISSUE

Right at quitting time Thursday we'd had a call from Emory O'Connor, the real estate fellow in Manchester whose company managed the Russians' house. One of the owners, or somebody working for the owners, had been to the house that day.

"I'm afraid there's an issue," Mr. O'Connor said.

"I guess there is," I said. "I saw it. Whoever got in there about took down that whole wall."

"That isn't the issue. Can you meet us up there tomorrow?"

Us?

So Friday morning at nine, I was back in Grenada, on that mountain, on my way to get a look at some of those famous Russians.

Going up their million-dollar driveway, I thought, not for the first time, how differently rich and poor set on a piece of land. If there's harm done, nine times out of ten it's the rich who do it, not the poor. All my life, this mountainside up here had been the back of the back-country. Out of the way, steep, heavily wooded, it had been perfectly good boondocks: good for logging, good for hunting, good for bears and porcupines. As the ass end of creation, it had done very well.

A poor man, if he had settled in here, would have bought a quarter-acre lot right on the road and moved in a trailer or put up a plain little house. He wouldn't have been able to afford to do anything more. Then by and by, suppose his house burned or he moved his trailer, in two years, less, it would be as if he'd never been here at all.

A rich man is different. He can afford to do whatever he wants, so he does a lot. He does everything. He buys the whole mountain, he clears ten, twenty acres at the top, he gets in heavy equipment, builds a road a quarter-mile long to his house site, puts in ponds, walls, banks, berms. If there's a hill where he don't want a hill, he grades it; if there's a dip where he don't want a dip, he fills it. He changes the whole place, the whole land, so it's to his liking — and he changes it forever. He turns the ass end of creation into real estate. Maybe the bears and the porcupines are still there, but now they're his bears and his porcupines, in a way they never were the poor man's.

It's when the money moves in that the neighborhood goes to hell, it looks like to me. Have a rich man for your friend, if you can, but a poor man for your neighbor.

When I got to the house, I found two vehicles parked in front: a wagon that I took for O'Connor's, with Vermont plates, and a Mercedes limousine, New York plates, with a man the size of your woodshed standing beside the driver's door, waiting. I parked the truck and got down. The driver of the Mercedes — I guessed he was the driver — beckoned to me, and I went over to him. Without saying a word, he proceeded to pat me down. Patting people down is something I have done a fair amount of myself, and I know good work when I see it. This fellow knew his business. He went over me as though I'd just flown in from Damascus or Teheran, carrying a heavy suitcase that went *tick-tock*. When he got done, he nodded and pointed toward the house, so I passed him and went on in.

Inside were Emory O'Connor and two others, standing in a hall-way with a high ceiling. O'Connor I knew, a bit. We shook hands, and he introduced me to one of the others.

"This is Mr. Tracy, Sheriff," O'Connor said. "He's up from New York, from the insurer. Sheriff Wing."

"Logan Tracy," the insurance company's man said. He was a

heavy, kind of soft fellow who looked like a college football player gone to seed. He had on one of those leather jackets that cost a few hundred dollars and that New Yorkers and others seem to think make them look like country people. But what country?

I shook hands with Mr. Tracy and looked to the third man, but nobody offered to introduce me to him, then or ever, and he never spoke a word that day. He was another kind of thing altogether, it looked like. He wore a gray suit and a dark tie. His shoes were polished. His hair was long, coal black, and slicked down and combed back around his head. He wasn't trying to look like a country man. He wasn't trying to look like anything. Was he a Russian? He might have been. He might have been from Pluto. Where he was not from was anyplace near here or anyplace like here.

"This way, Sheriff," said Logan Tracy. He turned toward the room we had seen the other day, the study. I followed him. Emory O'Connor started to go with us, but Tracy told him to wait where he was, in the hall with the third man.

Somebody had picked up. The papers and other things that had been spilled over the desk and floor last Friday were put away. Tracy sat himself down on the edge of the desk and looked at me.

"This is a nice property, Sheriff," he said.

I nodded.

"The owners keep it as a getaway, you know?" he said. "They come up here to relax. They don't want a lot of activity or trouble. They certainly don't want police going over the place. They are here to relax and have fun."

"Who are the owners?" I asked him.

Tracy went on. "There are valuables in the house," he said. "You've seen some of them: TV, electronics, appliances. There are cameras, firearms. There are artworks."

"Is the gentleman in the other room one of the owners?"

"We have an inventory," Tracy said. "Everything is accounted for. Except one thing."

"What's that?"

The quiet, slick-haired fellow who had been waiting with O'Connor had come to the study. He stood in the doorway.

"A safe," Logan Tracy said. "A small, fireproof safe. Steel. It was in the bookcase, there."

"How small?"

Tracy held his hands in front of him, about a foot and a half apart. He looked over at the man in the doorway. The man nodded.

"It's a keyed safe," said Tracy. "It's strong, might weigh forty or fifty pounds. Still, easy enough to carry away."

"What was in it?"

"Records."

"Records?"

"Business records, Sheriff. Nothing of value to a common burglar. Nothing that could be sold. Records."

"What kind of records?"

"Look, Sheriff," said Tracy. "I've told you that's irrelevant. The point is, these things have no value."

"But the owners want them back," I said. "They want them back pretty bad."

"They do," said Tracy. "Have you been investigating this, at all, Sheriff?"

"I've asked around."

"You've asked around. Have you asked Sean Duke? Our information is that somebody called Sean Duke did this. Do you know him?"

"Where do you get your information?" I asked Tracy.

"That's no concern of yours, Sheriff," he said. "Do you know Duke?"

"Sure."

"Is he the breaker?"

"I don't know."

"Is he your main suspect?"

"I wouldn't say that."

"Have you questioned him?"

"Not yet. Have you?"

"What do you mean, Sheriff?"

"Somebody else was up here looking for Sean Duke a few days back," I said. "Found him, too. Might have wished he hadn't. Fellow from Russia. Fellow named Eugene."

"I know nothing about that, Sheriff," said Tracy.

"Does he?" I looked over at the man in the doorway.

"No," said Logan Tracy.

"How tough would your safe be to get into?" I asked Tracy.

Tracy looked at the man in the doorway, who shook his head slightly.

"Tough," said Tracy.

"Then it's likely whoever took it threw it away," I said.

"Would you be apt to find it, then?"

"Depends on where they threw it."

"Look, Sheriff," said Tracy. "I'm not going to spar with you. That gets us nowhere. Let's be clear, shall we? Somebody broke in here and robbed us. Maybe you know who it was, maybe you don't. It doesn't matter. We want him caught. That's what you do. We're on the same side, here."

"We are?"

Tracy stood up from the desk where he had been sitting. "Alright,

Sheriff," he said, "This isn't useful. We'll leave it. The owners do want their property restored, obviously. That's your job. I'm sure we can count on you, can't we? Let me say, the owners are in a position to offer a reward for the return of their property. A substantial reward. Maybe that will help you in your investigation."

"I work for the county," I said.

"Of course you do, Sheriff," said Tracy. "We appreciate that. I'm only saying the owners are prepared to be helpful to those who are helpful to them. You understand, I'm sure."

"You're right," I said. "I do understand."

Tracy pulled a card out of his pocket and handed it to me. "You'll keep me informed," he said.

"Are there going to be more fellows like that Eugene coming around?" I asked.

"I told you, Sheriff," said Logan Tracy, "I don't know anything about anybody by that name."

I took a look at Tracy's card. It had his name on it, and in the corner the name Atlantic Casualty, and a telephone number. There was no street address.

"Where is your office?" I asked Tracy.

"How do you mean?"

"How do I mean?" I said. "How do *you* mean? There's no address here. On your card. No address. Where's your office?"

"New York."

"New York's a big place," I said.

"We're downtown," Tracy said.

He started toward the door of the study. The man who had been standing there had gone. Emory O'Connor had left too, it looked like. He wasn't in the hall where he'd been waiting, and when I left the house, his car wasn't there.

Did I enjoy being talked to like the dumbest boy in the third grade by that fellow with his fancy leather jacket and his little business card that not even the dumbest boy in the third grade would believe? Not really. But I don't mind. In sheriffing, you ain't there to show everybody you're the smartest fellow in the room. You're there to do your job, and sometimes you do it better if you look ten degrees cooler in the top story than you really are. That way, instead of talking, you shut up and listen, and watch. That way, you ask dumb questions, and sometimes it's the answers to the dumb questions that are interesting — and the no-answers.

So no, I didn't mind Mr. Tracy. Wingate used to say: Everybody thinks you've got to come out on top. You don't. All you've got to do is do your job.

That was pure Wingate. On sheriffing he ran a kind of — what is it where everybody sits around and asks questions and nobody ever answers them? A seminar. Wingate ran a kind of a seminar on sheriffing. The end was always the same: do your job. All you have to do is do your job. But Wingate never said what the job was. You were supposed to figure that out on your own. On your own, but Wingate's way.

———

Deputy Keen was at the office when I got back from the Russians' house. He had talked to the Sweetheart of Sigma Chi about Sean. It sounded like he'd had better luck with her than I did.

"She ain't a bad kid, Sheriff," the deputy said. "Fucking Superboy's got her brainwashed."

"Does she say where he is?"

"No," said Lyle. "She don't know where he is. She don't even see that much of him. He don't really live there, with her. He checks in every few days with a case of beer and a bunch of dope, and they, you know, they get it on all day and all night. Then he takes off. She thinks he's going to marry her."

"Is that what she says?"

"She don't have to say it. She's only just eighteen, you know. She's had a tough time. Her dad hit on her; when he wasn't hitting on her he was beating her up. She didn't finish school. Working at Wendy's, there. One shithead guy after another. She's going nowhere, and she knows it. Here comes Superboy. He's got a job, he's got a little money in his pocket. Sometimes he'll change his socks, take a shower, even. He looks good to Crystal."

"I guess he does."

"She's a good kid," Lyle went on. "She loves that big dog. Jackson. What a monster. Did you see him? I don't know why she calls him Jackson. I'll have to ask her. I'm going back out there later, see she's okay. She could use a break, you know? And instead she gets Superboy. That little toad. I'd like to — "

"Okay, Deputy, that'll do," I said.

"Well, Sheriff?" Lyle said. "Well? What? You know as well as I do it was Superboy broke into that place. We ought to just go ahead and bust him."

"We can't bust him for what I know as well as you do but maybe ain't true," I said. "We can't bust him for what neither one of us can prove. Maybe them Russians could, if they were at home, but we can't."

"*You* can't," said Deputy Keen.

"You, neither," I said, "as long as I'm sheriff."

"As long as you're sheriff."

"As long as I'm sheriff," I said again.

"As long."

"And, plus," I said, "we can't bust him if we can't find him."

"Well, I'll give you that," said Deputy Keen. "But we'll find him. I'll find him."

———

The deputy left, and I sat there and thought things over — didn't get far with it, though. I decided I didn't yet have quite enough to think about to make thinking worthwhile. So I got on my legs and went across the street to Addison's office, there in back of the courthouse. Let's get some more players on the field, here.

I found Addison standing at the window, looking out. He was wearing his wide red suspenders and a blue bow tie. The country lawyer. All Addison needed was the corncob pipe, and he has a couple of them, too.

"There is a kid down there cutting the grass who I believe must be asleep," said Addison when I came in. "Asleep or drunk. Look at him." He pointed out the window. Leo Crocker, on his little tractor, was mowing the lawn beside the courthouse.

"That's Leo," I said. "What's the matter with him?"

"He's missing half the lawn," said Addison. "He's leaving big strips between his cuts. Place is going to look like a god damned corn maze. Leo Who? Is he one of your guys?"

"No, sir," I said. "My guys don't cut the grass."

"I know they don't, Lucian," said Addison. "Sit down. How's our favorite little girl?" He sat behind his desk. I stood.

"Who do you mean?" I asked him.

"Hah," said Addison. "Hah, hah. A hit, Lucian. A very palpable hit. We'll make a comic out of you yet. What can I do for you?"

"You can search a title for me," I said. I told him about the Russians' house, about the break-in.

"What town?" asked Addison. I told him the town the house was in. Addison was making notes.

"New house?" he asked.

"Pretty. Last five years, I'd guess."

"What else?"

"Emory O'Connor manages it," I said. "Probably sold it, too."

"And you want to know who's owned it?"

"I want to know who owns it now."

"Ask Emory," said Addison.

"I will," I said. "I'm asking you, too. I like asking people things."

Addison smiled faintly and nodded. "Going to cost you," he said. Now we're getting to the fun part.

"Come on," I said. "You're assisting a county officer in the performance of his duty. That's pro bono."

"The hell it is," Addison grinned. "You know what pro bono means in Latin, don't you, Lucian?"

I shook my head.

"It means, 'For suckers,'" said Addison.

SHERIFFING II

"We'll find him," says the deputy. Then he says, "I'll find him." He might do it, too. Lyle's sharp, he works hard, and he's got incentive. He's got incentive because if people see Lyle putting in the hours, the days, to apprehend an evildoer, if they get the idea that he's a worker (if, along the way, they maybe get the idea he's a good deal harder a worker than his boss) — well, that suits Lyle, too.

It suits him because of the election. Hear how he said, "As long?" There's an election coming up. There's always an election coming up. Now, I was saying earlier, that means everybody reckons they've got a handle on the sheriff in a way they don't on other cops; it means they want to see you doing your job, every day. That's so, they do. But it can also mean that if they see you, they're happy. Whether you're really doing the job or not don't matter as much as being seen doing it does.

That don't make sense, does it? No, it don't. Come to that, electing the sheriff don't make sense. It ain't that kind of job. A couple of hundred people climb onto an airliner and are waiting to take off. Do they get to have an election to decide who's going to be pilot? Do they get to pick the one who looks best in a pilot uniform, the one who sounds best on the radio? No. Somebody else decides who's the pilot, and the passengers like it — or they get off the plane.

It looks to me like electing the sheriff is like electing the pilot. Don't misunderstand: I ain't against elections. Majority rules.

Democracy's a wonderful thing. But from time to time we take it right out the window.

Clemmie says thinking that way makes me some kind of a Nazi, some kind of a storm trooper. We've gone a few rounds on that one, too.

"Do I look like a storm trooper to you?" I ask her.

"No," says Clemmie, "you don't look like one, but you think like one. That's worse."

"It is?"

"Mister Law. You think you are the law. You think you and the law are the same."

"I do?"

"Shut up," says Clemmie.

"I didn't say nothing."

"I know you didn't," says Clemmie. "Shut up."

"Wait, now," I say. "Wait, now. Let's see. You reckon I think I'm the law, but, let's see. What is the law? Who does the law come from? It comes from the people, don't it?"

"I suppose so."

"You suppose so. I suppose so, too. How?"

"How, what?"

"How do the people decide what laws to have? Elections, ain't it?"

"I suppose so."

"You suppose right. Elections. You're going great, here. Okay, we'll take the next one real slow. How did I get my job? I was elected, wasn't I? I seem to recall being elected. Sure, I was. The people elected me."

I reckon I've tagged her there. But I get to sleep on the couch, just the same, and then next morning I get to look at her back again. Clemmie may take life too seriously, sometimes.

— 63 —

All I'm saying is about sheriffing. Democracy makes sheriffing harder, and easier. It makes doing the job harder and holding the job easier — or maybe it's the other way around.

'Course, a lot depends on what you think the job is.

———

One day when I'd been sheriff's deputy for six months or so and was getting to feel like I could handle the work, Wingate gave me a court writ of some kind for a fellow named Chalmers Babcock, who everybody called Chum.

Chalmers Babcock sounds like the name of a high flier. Chum was anything but. He must have been eighty at the time. He and his wife lived way to hell out in the woods in West Gilead: no plumbing, no electric. Chum got by picking ferns and trapping muskrats and working at the sawmill in the winter. I don't recall what kind of trouble he was in that had led to him being served, but it was nothing unusual. Chum was in and out of court quite a lot. If it hadn't been for having to go to court, he'd never have got to town at all, it looked like.

So it was that I took the writ and set out for West Gilead on a fine warm day in May with dandelions in the meadows and the little shadbushes coming out pink and white along the roads. Yes, the dandelions were out and the shadblow, too — and right along with them, sure enough, the blackflies were as thick as you ever see them. When I got out of the patrol car at Chum's, far back in the middle of the woods as he was, the flies were worse. I mean, they were right there, swarming around my head and face like a cloud of poison gas.

Chum's wife was waiting for me in the dooryard. She wore one of those headdresses made of black mosquito netting to keep the bugs off, so you couldn't see her face. She looked like an Arab woman.

"Mrs. Babcock?" I said. "Is Mr. Babcock here?"

I was taking it slow, you see. In process serving, of course, you have to have the customer in person, in front of you. You have to serve his face, as they say. We all knew that. Chum wasn't going to make it easy.

"He's upstairs," said Mrs. Babcock.

Behind her, over the door of their house, was an open window.

"Mr. Babcock?" I called out. The blackflies were crawling around in my hair, they were crawling down my collar, up my nose, they were buzzing in my eyes, in my ears.

Something came flying out of the upstairs window and landed at my feet. It was a glass Mason jar, a canning jar, held about a pint. It didn't break, but it lay there in a pool of what had been in it — a yellow liquid that might have been flat beer. It wasn't flat beer.

"Mr. Babcock?" I called. "It's Deputy Wing. From the sheriff's. I need to talk to you." I flapped and flailed and batted around my head at the cloud of bugs.

"I know who you are," said Chum from inside, but he stayed back from the window so I couldn't see him. Another Mason jar came out the window. It hit the ground and broke, and what was in it splashed over Mrs. Babcock's and my shoes. I took a step back from the house.

"Mr. Babcock?" I called. "Chum?"

"I ain't saying so. You didn't hear me say it's me," said Chum. "I know who you are and I know why you're here. You've got another god damned summons, don't you?"

Then I thought I had an idea.

"Yes, sir, I do," I said. "I do have a summons. Mr. Babcock, the bugs are awful out here. Can I come inside?"

"Heh, heh," said Chum. "Hell, no, you can't come inside." A third jar flew out the window and broke against my patrol car.

"How many jars has he got up there?" I asked Mrs. Babcock.

"Quite a few, it looks like," she said. "He knew you'd be along. He's been saving up."

"Bugs are pretty savage today, ain't they?" called Chum from inside. "You don't want to be standing around out there. Here's what you do. Put your summons away, get back in your rig, go home, and tell Ripley Wingate he can take his summons, stick it up his ass, and bust it off."

Nobody had anything to say to that. Mrs. Babcock turned to me. "Let me see your paper," she said.

I handed the writ to her. She took it out of its envelope, raised her bug veil, read the summons. She stuck it back into its envelope.

"This ain't going to work," she said. "He ain't going to take it. You'd better go."

"What about the writ?"

"Leave your paper with me," said Mrs. Babcock. "I'll see he gets it."

"You know I can't do that, Mrs. Babcock," I said.

"Well," she said, "you'd better go, then." She handed me the summons.

I went back to the department and told Wingate I couldn't serve Chum.

" 'Course you couldn't," said Wingate.

I told him the circumstances: the blackflies, Mrs. Babcock, the Mason jars, what was in the Mason jars, the upper window. Wingate nodded.

"We'll give him another whirl in a day or two," said Wingate.

"A day or two? Why not now?"

Wingate seemed to think about this, and then, "No," he said. "We'll let him work, we'll let him develop for a little."

So it was a couple of days later that Wingate and I went out to Babcocks' together. We had our writ, and this time each of us had his own anti-bug headgear — county issue. We found Mrs. Babcock out front, and the three of us were standing there in our black veils like a club of beekeepers getting ready to go to a funeral, when here comes Chum out of the house in his own bug net, a specially heavy, dark, long one, and he starts right in on Wingate.

"Sent the big boy today, I see," said Chum. He was having a fine time. "You've got your paper with you, I guess."

"We've got it," said Wingate.

"This is a dogshit business, here, Sheriff," said Chum. "I never moved that son of a bitch's stakes. Why would I?"

"I didn't say you did," said Wingate. "I ain't here to say one way or another what anybody did. I'm here to serve you."

"You can't."

"Why not?"

"You don't know who you're serving," said Chum, very pleased with himself. "A man wouldn't know his own mother if she was wearing one of these." He tugged at the black bug veil, which hung down to his chest. "You can't prove who I am. You can't serve me."

At that I felt my blood pressure starting to climb. Here's Chum, living out in the woods like a rabid coon, more than half crazy, pissing into fruit jars to throw at public servants, by now well into his second day of wasting the sheriff's time and the taxpayers' money over a two-dollar lawsuit with the rabid coon down the road, who's as crazy as he is — and he thinks he can come over like some crafty lawyer in a pin-striped suit. I wanted to cuff him and take him in to the lockup.

Wingate knew it, too. He knew how I felt. He put his hand on my shoulder for a second and leaned toward Chum a little, like he was trying to see through Chum's blackfly veil. He shook his head.

"You're right," said Wingate. "I couldn't swear it was you. It looks like you got us, Chum."

"Hah. Very clever," said Chum. "But I ain't saying nothing to that, am I? I ain't answering like it's me. You can't prove it's me."

"It looks like we'll have to go back to the clerk and advise him, we'll have to tell him it ain't been served," said Wingate. He handed the summons in its envelope to me.

"Put it in the car," said Wingate.

I went to our patrol car and put the summons on the dash, then returned to Wingate and the two Babcocks. Wingate was talking to Mrs. Babcock.

"I saw Lucinda the other day," he told her. "How is she doing?" Lucinda was Mrs. Babcock's big sister. She had come out of the hospital after having a female operation.

"She don't seem to rally," said Mrs. Babcock. "She don't have any energy."

"I know it," said Wingate.

"Lucy ain't young," said Mrs. Babcock.

"I know it," said Wingate.

"None of us is," said Mrs. Babcock.

"I know it," said Wingate.

We got in the patrol car and started back to the office. There, Wingate took out the summons, signed it, and handed it to me.

"Just take it across and give it to the clerk," he said. "Tell him it's served."

"But it ain't," I said.

"Yes, it is," said Wingate. "Chum knows where he has to be. He knows when. If he don't, *she* does. Chum will show up. She'll drag him in by his ear if she has to."

That was, oh, twenty-five, thirty years ago. Chum and Mrs. Chum are under the grass. Wingate's over eighty, and I ain't exactly green in the sap, myself. That business with Chum was sheriffing the way I was learning to do it from Wingate. Sometimes you have to hold back and let a thing develop, was one of his rules.

It's still good, too. It's a good rule. But a kid like Sean tests it. Yes, he does. An old fool like Chum, you can let him develop and things will get better. He'll come around, or if he don't his wife will make him. You know that. With Sean, if you let him develop, you don't know. Things may get better. They may get worse.

9

BIG LOOKERS ON THE DOWNSIDE

Saturday is no day off for the sheriff. Evildoers, the unlucky, and our most faithful customers, the plain rock-stupid, are generally open for business well before noon, and then of course you build through the day Saturday to your big night of the week for bad behavior.

I thought I'd give myself a ride over to Manchester that Saturday and have a visit with Emory O'Connor, see if I couldn't get some kind of an idea about who it was we were dealing with at the Russians' place. Then later on, I meant to poke around here and there, try to start Sean out of whatever hole he'd gone down. Deputy Keen, I guessed, would be doing the same.

I was pretty sure Emory would be working, too. Saturday is a busy day in the real estate business, as in sheriffing. Is that because home buyers forget for the weekend that they're going to have to work to earn the money to pay off all the debt they're about to go into? I don't know.

Emory O'Connor did very well. He had his office in a nice old brick house right on the green in Manchester. He'd bought the place and spent a lot of money in fixing it up so it looked right, or a little better than right. Emory liked to make money, and he liked to spend money — and he was good at both.

He was in his reception room talking on the phone when I walked in. He wasn't happy to see me, but he held his hand up for me to wait, and when he got done with his call we went into his office and he shut the door. Emory took the chair behind his desk, and I sat across the desk from him.

"What can I do for you this morning, Sheriff?" Emory asked me.

"Well," I said, "you can tell me who in the world is that fellow Tracy, at the place up in Grenada, who's his friend with the slicked-down hair who don't have much to say, who's behind them. You can start by doing that for me."

Emory smiled and shook his head. "No, I can't, Sheriff," he said. "Not really. You know as much as I do. Tracy's with the owners' insurance company, in New York. I told you that. The other guy's name I don't know, either. I took it he's one of the owners or their representative."

"Buster Mayhew, your caretaker, says the owners ain't around much. He says they're some kind of foreigners. He can't understand what they're saying."

Emory chuckled. "If you've talked to Buster," he said, "you know he may not be the brightest guy who ever lived. He's paid to make sure the doors are locked, basically. He's not paid to be a linguist, Sheriff. He doesn't have to talk to the owners."

"You do, though. Who are the owners?"

"Investors," said Emory.

"Investors," I said. "There's a good many investors, one kind and another, here and there, ain't there? Do these ones have names? They pay you, don't they? For managing the place? Somebody sends you checks."

Emory smiled again. "Oh, yes," he said. "Big ones."

"Who's name's on the checks?"

"Odessa Partners, Limited," said Emory. He was sounding a little short.

"Who are they?"

Emory shrugged. "Investors," he said.

"Where are they located?"

"Offshore."

Getting information out of Emory was like trying to get a turtle to stick its head out of its shell when you've caught it crossing the road.

"Offshore, where?"

"St. George's, Bermuda," said Emory.

"Bermuda?"

"Does that surprise you, Sheriff?" said Emory. "Bermuda's a very — I guess *hospitable* is the word. It's a very hospitable place."

"They're Russians," I said. "At the house in Grenada. They ain't Bermudas. The place is full of papers in Russian, newspapers, magazines. They've even got Russian skin books. Bermuda? Do they read Russian in Bermuda?"

"Look, Sheriff," said Emory. "I'm not responsible for what they read. Bermuda's where the checks come from. Have for several years. Very regular. Very useful. We're in business, here, you know."

"I know you are," I said. "I know you're in business. And, talking about business, that insurance company in New York? Atlantic Casualty? Mr. Tracy's company? That's a business, too, ain't it?"

"Of course it is."

" 'Course it is," I said. "But it's the damndest thing. What would you say if I told you I called New York, and the telephone company down there never heard of Atlantic Casualty? There ain't no such business."

"If you're asking me whether that surprises me," said Emory, "I have to tell you I can't say it does."

"Don't it kind of trouble you, though?"

"Not in the least," said Emory.

"There ain't much does, is there?" I asked him.

"Look, Sheriff," said Emory. "What do you want from me here?

I'm in the real estate business. I'm not in the business of morality checks. Do I think Logan Tracy is a Sunday school teacher on vacation? No. Do I think Odessa Partners buys guide dogs for blind children? No. Do I care? No."

Look, Sheriff, says Emory. *Look, Sheriff*, says Logan Tracy. Look, this. Look, that. Your big lookers, these important fellows are. When you hear that "Look," be careful. Go slow. Because the fellow who's telling you to look don't want you to. He wants you to think he's an honest, plain-talking straight shooter who, when he says "Look," is getting ready to level with you. He ain't. He never is. He says *look*, but he means *don't look*.

"Do you follow me, Sheriff?" Emory asked. "I'm telling you that you know as much as I do here. I can't help you. Much as I'd like to, I can't. Now, I know how busy you are."

"I ain't busy. I ain't at all busy. Take your time. I've got all day."

"You do, maybe, Sheriff. I don't. Can we wrap this up?"

I got up from my chair. Emory stayed sitting behind his desk. He didn't offer to shake hands.

"Have a nice day, Sheriff," he said.

Well, I might have lost Emory's vote there. Couldn't be helped. No hard feelings on my end, though. Emory's a businessman, sure he is. He's in the real estate business. That means he's a valuable man. The real estate business is big in these parts, and getting bigger. On the whole, that's a good thing. Now, to be sure, it does bring in people like Emory, it brings in your big lookers, people with a very high opinion of themselves based on what, when you take away their money, it ain't always easy to see. The big lookers are the — what do you call the bad part of the good part? They're the downside. Are ten thousand Emory O'Connors a downside? You bet they are.

But still and all, I say thank God for real estate. Because it looks like real estate is about the only thing we've got left up here that people are willing to spend serious money on. Other good things people used to get from us, like milk, cows, tool and die work, lumber, sheep, saddle horses, wool, and the rest they're getting from someplace else, but real estate's something people want that we've still got plenty of. We're adding more, too, every day, and we're selling the hell out of it. It looks as though there's no bottom to real estate.

————

At the department I had a note from Clemmie to call her dad. Was I making Addison work on Saturday? If so, we might be into something. Addison generally preferred to devote his weekend to toddy.

"It's about your title search," Addison said when I reached him.

"I've gotten a little farther with that, too," I said.

"Farther, how?"

"Sat down with Emory this morning," I said. "Emory says the owner of the place is some kind of investment company, I guess, in Bermuda. Odessa. Odessa Partners."

"Well," said Addison. "Yes. Odessa is part of it. Odessa is the Cub Scouts. They still had the training wheels on when they set up Odessa."

"Training wheels?"

"Stop by the office Monday," said Addison. "Or, no. Lucian? Come to the house. Come now."

I drove out toward Devon, and at Addison's I went right to the back of the house and came in through the kitchen. Addison was there, making a pot of coffee. He poured a cup for each of us, then uncorked the big jug of White Horse Scotch that he likes to keep ready to hand at all times. He held the bottle over my cup; I shook my head. Addison poured a shot into his coffee.

"I need this, don't you know," he said. "You and your god damned title search."

We sat at the kitchen table, where Addison had laid out a folder full of yellow legal notepaper. He patted the folder.

"I can write all this up for you, if that's what you want," he said. "There'd be no point. And I won't try to go through it now. We'd both go to sleep. You've got a Russian novel, here."

"I never read a Russian novel," I said. "I don't know what you're talking about."

"Thousands of pages, hundreds of people, all with the same names, in places with the same names, doing the same things. That's a Russian novel."

"Okay," I said.

Addison took a hit of his coffee.

"I didn't get far searching the title at the town hall in Grenada," he began. "I got to Odessa Partners. Then I came back here and got to work on them. Chased them from Bermuda on down into the Caymans and through the Caribbean, pillar to post, like a god damned booze cruise. Wound up in Amsterdam."

"Amsterdam?"

"A Dutch company. I thought, *Hmm*. So I called an old class-mate of mine. He works in The Hague. I'm not sure what he does, exactly, or who he is. Hell, I'm not even sure he knows who he is anymore. But he knew all about the Dutch company. He gave me some advice."

"What was that?"

"Forget it. Drop it. Turn the page. Walk away. Move on."

"Why?"

"I haven't followed the thing all the way," said Addison. "I don't know that I could, come to that, or that my classmate could. Doesn't matter. I'm out of it. So should you be. Your burglarized house is the property of people overseas who operate mostly in Russia, the Baltic, and on south: the Caucasus, Iran. Serious places, Lucian. Wide open places, these days. Good places to stay away from. Serious people, too — also good to stay away from."

"What do they do?"

"They keep busy. They're a gifted people, the Russians, but they do nothing by halves. And also, of course, they're all quite mad. The Russians, don't you know, have a claim to be the fourth-craziest people on earth, after ourselves, the Japanese, and the French — and I'm not sure they might not have the edge of the French, in an impartial trial.

"These people in Grenada," Addison went on, "are in the energy field, mainly. Don't ask me exactly what that means. I don't know. But being in the energy field where they are today is like being in the bootleg liquor field used to be in, say, Chicago. You know what I mean?"

"I know what you mean," I said. "Why drop it?"

"Why not?" asked Addison. "You don't have a dog in this fight, do you? Your office doesn't, not really. Somebody scoped a place out, broke in, did some damage, left. So what? Happens every day."

"There's more," I said. I told Addison about Sean, the missing strongbox, the Russian fellow Sean had taken down.

"Sean Duke?" Addison asked.

"You know him?"

"Everybody knows Sean Duke."

"Everybody?"

"Everybody, Lucian," said Addison. "He's a popular young man. Come on, have a little one, here." He pushed the jug toward me, but I didn't want any. Addison took it back and gave himself another pop.

"If you find him," Addison said, "Sean, you get him out of here. If he's got something these people want, well . . . Do they know he's got it?"

"They sent that Russian fellow to get it back."

"You don't know they did."

"House full of Russians gets broken into. Couple of days later, here comes another Russian looking for the breaker. That's a lot of Russians. This ain't Moscow."

Addison nodded. "Well," he said, "you get your boy out of here, that's all."

"My boy?" I said. "He ain't my boy."

"Are you sure?"

"I'm sure."

"Get him out, all the same," said Addison. "Put him away someplace."

"The way he's going," I said, "I won't be the one puts him away. The state will."

"No," said Addison. "That's no good. That's jail. If he's in jail, that's serving him up to these people on a platter with an apple in his mouth. He needs to be gone, Lucian. Make him go."

"I've got to find him first."

"I can't help you there. What was in the box he took?"

"Records, the fellow said. Business records."

"Right," said Addison. He sipped his coffee — if any of what he had left in his cup was coffee.

"Cossacks," said Addison.

"Who?"

"Cossacks. You'd better catch up with this boy, don't you know, Lucian? You'd better catch up with him before the Cossacks do. God damned Cossacks."

———

I found Morgan Endor on the back road in Mount Zion that comes down from the ski resort on Stratton Mountain. It wasn't a fancy place: no Russians' house. She was in the kind of house the builders used to call a chalet, back when the ski promoters wanted you to believe you were getting, I guess, Switzerland in Vermont for your money instead of Las Vegas in Vermont, like today.

She opened the door to my knock and stood there in the doorway, looking at me as though she didn't know who I was, or maybe I was the fellow pumped out the septic tank but she hadn't called the fellow pumped out the septic tank.

"Sheriff," she said.

"That's right, Ms. Endor," I said. "Can I come in? I won't be long. I'm still looking for Sean."

"He's not here."

"I know."

She stood back so I could walk in.

Inside was a long room with a stone fireplace at one end and windows looking south over the mountains. The sun was in the windows, and a big tabby cat was asleep in the sun on the carpet. The cat didn't offer to move when we walked in. We had to step around it.

"That's a calm cat," I said.

Morgan Endor looked down at the cat as though she hadn't noticed it till now.

"Is it?" she said. "I suppose it is. It belongs to my parents, actually."

She sat on a couch facing the windows. In that strong light she looked older than I'd thought she was when she came to the office — nearer forty-five than thirty-five. She was starting to have lines at the corners of her eyes, and her neck was getting lean. Sean wasn't exactly robbing the cradle this time, it didn't look like.

"I won't lie to you, Sheriff," said Morgan Endor. "Sean's been here. He was here last night. I told him you wanted to see him. I told him you thought he was in some kind of trouble. He laughed."

"What time did he leave?" I asked her.

"About eight."

"That's eight last night?"

"Eight this morning, Sheriff."

"Where was he going when he left?"

"I don't know."

"Ms. Endor," I said, "here's what we're up to in this thing. Sean's been working at a big house over in Grenada. It's a vacation place. Nobody's there, mostly. We think Sean broke into the house looking for valuables."

Morgan Endor was looking at me. She raised her eyebrows a little. "Go on, Sheriff," she said.

"We know Sean," I said. "We know he ain't the Young Republicans. We know he was working at the place. He knew the setup there: nobody home, no neighbors, rich people with lots of goods. We know he knew the house was burglar alarmed, but we also know he knew it's so far out in the woods that he'd have all kinds of time to go through it between when the alarm went off and any law could get there. He wouldn't have to worry about getting around the alarm: he could just bust his way in, which is what he did."

"Suppose he did. Why tell me?"

"You're his friend."

"I didn't say that. I said he was an acquaintance."

"So you did. And I said I needed to talk to him, that he was in trouble. I still do. He still is."

"Is he?" she asked. "I wonder. Can you prove any of the things you've told me?"

"No," I said. "I can't. That's the thing. Sean ain't in trouble from me, not really, because I can't go after him without proof. But there are other people in this thing, too, and they can do whatever they want."

"What other people?"

"People who own the house Sean busted into."

"Who are they?"

"I don't know for sure. I've been trying to find out. But they are very bad news, I know that. They know Sean went into their place. If they catch up with him, they won't need proof to do what they have to do. Do you see what I'm saying?"

"Yes, Sheriff, I see. But even if you're right about Sean, it's for the police to act. It's for you. Why would these people think they had to do anything?"

"Because Sean took something from their house. A kind of a little safe or strongbox, I guess. They're not in a hurry for the police to get their hands on it, but they're ready to go some way to get it back, it looks like, or what's in it. They're ready to go a long way. You don't know about anything like that?"

"Certainly not," said Morgan Endor. "What was in it that's so valuable to your people?"

"They ain't my people," I said. "I don't know what was in it. They don't say."

"You think the man Sean fought was from these people?"

"That's what I think."

She smiled then. "Sean didn't seem to have much trouble with that one, though, did he? I gathered you found him tied to a tree naked. Sean handled him, didn't he?"

"Sean was lucky," I said.

"Sean's a lucky young man."

"You think so?"

"I think you worry too much about him."

"About Sean? I don't worry about Sean. I'm doing my job."

"Is that what you're doing, Sheriff?"'

"That's what I'm doing."

"Well," she said. "Maybe you worry too much about those other people, then."

"I don't think so," I said. "I saw the fellow. I saw the gun he had on him, too. So did you. I worry about fellows who carry guns. Don't you?"

She shrugged.

"I worry about them because there's apt to be more than one to a litter," I said.

Morgan Endor smiled again. "Sean can take care of himself," she said.

Sean can take care of himself? Wrong. Not for a day, he can't, not for an hour. Sean can do a lot of things. He can fix your roof. He can pick up a two-hundred-pound flowerpot and toss it through your patio door. He can steal your strongbox. He can mop the floor with your imported evildoer. He can go all night putting the old inner life to his lady photographer in her chalet, get up, cup of coffee, slide right down to the trailer park and roll the doughnut with the Sweetheart of Sigma Chi. Sean can do all those things. But take care of himself, he cannot.

Morgan Endor thought he could, or she said she did. She was wrong if she thought so. But she didn't look like she was often wrong about things. I didn't get Morgan Endor. I didn't get her name, I didn't get her age. I didn't get her when she came to the office with the Russian's pants, and I still didn't get her. I couldn't figure her out. In sheriffing, that happens, too. You don't always figure everybody out. There are some people you never do get.

———

Driving home that evening, I thought about Addison and his Russian novels. Good old Addison, always holding a ticket you don't have. Well, whoever these Grenada Russians were, they weren't in no novel, and they had Addison's attention, it looked like. He was more than a little spooked.

Or maybe it was the White Horse. I wondered whether or not I should tell Clemmie that her dad might be working the stuff a little harder than usual. Would telling her about it make anything better? I about decided no, I'd shut up. But then it didn't matter, because when I got home, Clemmie wasn't there.

10

THE COSSACKS

Late that Sunday night, Monday morning, the balloon went up. It went up about halfway. Errol called me at home after three to say he'd had a trouble call from Monterey for a disturbance at one of the trailers there, the Finn trailer: a fight or a party, it looked like to Errol, or, more likely, both at once. He'd gotten Deputy Keen, who was patrolling, on the radio, and Lyle had started over there. Then a couple of minutes later Errol had gotten a second call, same place, saying shots had been fired. That's when he called me.

I got there about quarter to four. Errol must have hit every switch on his desk, because we lacked nobody at the scene except the Salvation Army. I saw state troopers, deputies of mine, medics, volunteer firemen, and two animal control officers from Brattleboro.

They had lights from the vehicles playing over the side of the trailer and over the little yard in front. You could see the door had been forced in, and you could see glass all over the ground in the yard. There was some blood on the cement-block steps at the door. I went on into the trailer.

The Sweetheart of Sigma Chi was in there surrounded by police and medics. She was a little shaky, but mainly alright. She was wearing a bathrobe and drinking a beer, sitting on the divan telling her story for the tenth time.

Deputy Keen was with her. He came over to where I waited in the trailer door and nodded toward the yard. We went out there together, and the deputy filled me in.

I have to say it was quite a story. It seems Crystal Finn was innocently asleep in her trailer around three o'clock when she heard banging and crashing and woke to find two men beating down her door. Crystal wasn't the only one who woke up, though, and that was bad luck for the intruders, because the minute they got inside the trailer here comes Jackson, Crystal's two-hundred-pound bull mastiff–wolf–alligator hybrid, storming full tilt out of the bedroom and right at them. They turned and ran for their car, which was parked in front, with the dog all over them and behind the dog, Crystal wearing a little black nightie and carrying an old side-by-side Ithaca. The dog grabs the hindmost fellow by the arm and commences to eat, but the fellow breaks free and makes their car, just as the quicker one fires it up and starts to roll, which is when Crystal lets go on them with the Ithaca, first one barrel, then the other. She said she thinks she got the driver, but maybe not, because they took off and kept going. She's sure she blew out their rear window, though. A neighbor called the police, but it's all over. Crystal's fine. The dog's fine.

"She's something else, ain't she?" said Deputy Keen.

"She is," I said.

"They won't get far," said Lyle, "not wounded and with their back end all shot up."

"Do we know who they were?"

"More Russians, Sheriff. Look here."

The deputy and I went to one of the state police cruisers, and he opened the door. Lying on the passenger's seat was a large, clear-plastic evidence envelope with some kind of cloth or fabric inside.

"That's part of the one fellow's coat," said Lyle. "Jackson ripped it away when he grabbed hold of the guy's arm. There's an inside pocket with a passport, French passport, in the name of Vaseline something."

"Vaseline?"

"Vaseline, Sheriff. Russian name. Plus, there are stamps in Russian all over the inside of it, the passport. I found the coat in the yard when I got here. Gave it to the troopers. I was first on scene."

"You find anything else with the coat?" I asked him.

"Couple of fingers."

"Fingers?"

"Jackson had a pretty good grip on him, it looks like," said Lyle.

"Was Sean here with the young lady, when these fellows showed up?" I asked.

"Crystal says no," said Deputy Keen. "And that brings me back to where I've been right along, Sheriff: Sean Duke. Superboy. When in hell are you going to get serious about him?"

"What's he got to do with this, here? It wasn't Sean did this tonight."

"It was because of him it happened," said Lyle. "They came here to find him. He's the reason they're here. You know that as well as I do."

"You're right," I said. "I do know that as well as you do. I also know if these fellows that were here find Sean before we do, we never will find him. There won't be nothing left to find."

"Suits me," said the deputy.

"Well, it don't suit me," I said.

"What are you more interested in, here, Sheriff?" the deputy asked me. "Solving a crime, a crime you know was committed by Superboy, or keeping the Russians off him? Which one?"

"Both."

"I don't figure that, Sheriff."

"You don't have to figure it, Deputy," I said. "All you have to do is follow your orders."

"What orders?" said Lyle. "I got no orders. All I *want* is orders. All I want is for you to do your job or at least let me do mine. That means running down Superboy. Don't it? Don't it?"

Two of the other deputies and some of the medics who had been in the trailer had come out into the yard and were listening to Deputy Keen, who had raised his voice. I didn't want to get into something with him in front of an audience.

"It seems to me," I told the deputy, "that the job right now, today, is finding the two fellows who were here before they get clean back to Russia while we stand here pissing on each other's shoes. Wouldn't you think?"

"Whatever you say, Sheriff," said Deputy Keen.

"Why don't you go ahead and do that, then? You want an order? You got one. You want to do your job? Go do it."

Deputy Keen turned and, taking all the time he needed and maybe a little more, he walked to his vehicle. He drove off. Another satisfied customer. All the others standing around in front of the Sweetheart's trailer were looking at me. It was beginning to get light.

———

Believe it or not, we never found them. You'd think a pair of Russians, one of them with half his hand chewed off, the other maybe with gunshot wounds, driving a car with a blown-out rear window and its bodywork full of those big double-o buckshot holes, would tend to attract attention to themselves, wouldn't you? I would. But nobody ever caught up with either of them — or hasn't yet.

The one who lost his passport was traceable, of course.

Lieutenant Farabaugh, my window on the world of international evildoers, ran him down the same day. The passport holder was Vassily Karataev, born Riga, Latvia, 1969. Citizenship, French. He had the same kind of sheet as the nude male except that, plus having been arrested in every city in Europe, Vassily had also done time in New Delhi, India.

The passport meant Dwight also had a line on the car the two Cossacks drove. Vassily had rented it at Kennedy Airport in New York the day before they turned up on our field. But that was as far as anybody could get with the car. It had disappeared, too. It turned up most of two years later, abandoned in a parking lot on the river in Detroit. Nobody had thought much about it out there, I guess, maybe because half the cars in Detroit are full of blood and buckshot holes, just like the Cossacks'.

11

THE SEANS OF THIS WORLD

Addison said a smart thing one time. Well, he said smart things more than once: he's a smart fellow, as I hope I have made plain. But one time in particular I'm thinking of, when Clemmie and I found out we weren't going to be having any kids.

That was not an easy thing. We'd been married five, six years, working it in the usual way, not exactly trying to fetch at any special time, but expecting a kid would come along. It didn't happen. Finally Clemmie thought she'd go to the doctor, get herself checked out for fertility. She went. She aced: Clemmie's sitting on more eggs than your granny's Rhode Island Red.

That passed the ball to me. And sure enough, I was the problem. It turned out my sperms were a lot like the old-time hardscrabble Vermont hill farmers of my childhood: few in number, barely hanging on, and never learned to swim.

So, no kids. It took some getting used to. Looking back, it took more getting used to than either of us would have thought. There's no better way to learn what you want than to find out you can't have it. Things with us weren't going to be quite the way we'd thought they'd be. Did we talk that over a lot between us, at the time? Did we get straight with each other on what it meant, on how we felt about it? I don't remember that we did. For me, I guess I said to myself, well, that's the deal you've got: it is what it is. Clemmie? It might have been tougher for Clemmie — probably was. We're different people, ain't we, different kinds of people? That's what makes it interesting. That's what makes it fun when it's fun, but that's also what makes it hard when it's hard. The way I said, Clemmie can take life too seriously.

But I was saying about Addison. Maybe Clemmie and I didn't talk much about having kids or not, but everybody else did, including Clemmie's cousins. It was one day we were all sitting around after lunch at Addison's, talking about sperms and eggs and hormones and all that fascinating kind of thing, and one cousin speaks up and says, Well, have you considered adoption?

And Addison, who's probably got a leg pretty well up over the back of the White Horse by now, gives a big guffaw and says, "Why would they do that?" Then, looking at me, "He's already adopted the whole god damned county, don't you know?" Good old Addison.

So: Deputy Keen says I'm not doing my job, that I'm giving Sean a get-out-of-jail-free card. Am I? I guess I am. Is that because of what Addison said back then? Am I making Sean a special case? Am I going easy on him because I think he's one of my own? Never. Sean ain't mine. I don't want him; he don't want me. If I'm giving him some extra rope — and I am — it's because that's my method. That's sheriffing. In sheriffing you don't stop things from happening. You know you can't do that, mostly, so you don't try. People are going to do what they're going to do. You let things happen. "Let them come to you," said Wingate.

Your bad boys, he was talking about. Let your bad boys come to you. The idea is that you give them a little cover, so they have a little room to screw up, a little time to figure things out and come around. What you're aiming for is a taxpayer with a few good stories, a few memories that today make him shake his head, and not a convict sitting in a jail cell somewhere.

In working with your bad boys, you're also in the conservation business, in a manner of speaking, you're in the endangered species business; because bad boys are getting scarce, at least the old-fashioned kind like Sean are. It's like I said before: without the Seans of this world, it looks like the only young fellows we'd have in these parts would be bank clerks and sales representatives and fellows who work on computers — kids who want to grow up to be big lookers, kids who want grow up to be Logan Tracy and Emory O'Connor.

Sure, there are bad boys who test Wingate's method, who won't come to you, who will not shape up, not ever. Sean may be one of them. But you don't assume that. You try to use the method with Sean, too. At least you try until you get done trying. Then you come down onto the hard bottom of the law, the bedrock, the place where Deputy Keen wants to do business. Then you say that your job is to make the law work, to make it real, and in the end what makes the law real can only be one thing. If you're a trooper, you carry it on your hip; if you're a sheriff like Wingate, like me, you keep it locked up in your sock drawer. But you've got it, you know where it is, you know how to use it, you know you're allowed to use it, and so does everybody else.

Would Sean make us all come down onto that hard place? I didn't think he would. And this time, anyhow, I was right. Because as it happened, I didn't catch up with Sean. Sean caught up with me.

He did it fairly neat, too: got me out of the office and as off duty as I ever am. Dinnertime. Clemmie was making something in the kitchen and came up with not enough sugar. Would I make a sugar run? So I got in her little car and drove down to the store at the Four Corners. It was beginning to get dark. I parked in front of the store, went in, got the sugar, paid for it, came back out front, and climbed into the car to start home. Sean was sitting in the back. He was down kind of low, so I didn't know he was there till he spoke up.

"Evening, Sheriff," said Sean.

"Jesus."

"Take it easy, Sheriff."

"I might have shot you," I said.

"You ain't got no gun, though," said Sean.

"You don't know that."

"Everybody knows that. Drive around for a few minutes, okay, Sheriff?"

"Where to?"

"I don't give a fuck. Just drive. Go ahead."

I started the car, and we left the store and went right, away from the Four Corners and up the hill.

"Sheriff, I told you to keep them fucking spics off me," said Sean. "I wrote you a note about that. Didn't I? Didn't I say that?"

"You know I've got nothing to do to keep them off or put them on," I said. "If you want to get done with them, you'll help me."

"Bullshit," said Sean. "They came after my girl. They didn't have the balls to come after me, not after what I did to the one fucker. So they came after her. Well, fuck them. They can kiss my ass."

"You ain't listening to me," I said. "Do you know why they're looking for you?"

"I don't give a fuck," said Sean. "Let them find me. Bring them the fuck on."

Talking to Sean was like talking to a barking dog, except that any dog that's smart enough to bark is smarter than Sean.

"Okay," I said. "Were you there at her trailer when they came?"

"Fuck, no," said Sean. "I had been, you would have had a couple of dead spics."

"You keep on saying spics. Who do you think these people are, here?"

"What?"

"Who do you think's after you? Who broke into Crystal's, there?"

"The Mafia," said Sean. "Fucking Mafia. Ain't they?"

"No, they ain't. They're from overseas. They're Russians."

"Russians? Fucking Commies?"

"No. They ain't Commies anymore. They switched teams, a while back, it looks like."

"Fuckers."

"They're just like us now," I said. "They want what's theirs. You've got what's theirs."

"Fuck I do," said Sean.

I pulled off the road into a turnout and switched off the motor. We were right at the top of Paradise Hill, and you could see out over the country to the south and west, toward Gilead, the hills like waves on the ocean, one after another, spread out in the evening as the sun set and houselights began to come on in the valleys between the hills, here and there, some lights close, some miles off.

"Okay," I said to Sean. "You wanted to talk. Talk, then. Tell me what you took out of their place. Tell me where it is. Then I can help you. Maybe I can."

"I tell you fucking nothing," said Sean. "I know what happens, I do."

"Nothing happens," I said. "Not for that. Not now. You've got the upper hand here, remember? You came to me. We get done, I'll drop you wherever you say, and off you go."

"How do I know that?"

"Because I said it."

Sean was quiet for a minute. He was probably trying to think if he knew how to say something without saying "fuck." It took him a while, but he finally made it. He said, "It wasn't just me."

"Who else?"

"Her," said Sean. "Crystal."

"You and Crystal broke in there together?"

"That's what I'm telling you, ain't it?" said Sean. "It was her idea."

"What did you take away?" I asked him.

"Now, I ain't saying I didn't do nothing," Sean went on. "That it was Crystal that did it all, not me. Fuck no. I did it. I busted down their door. I'd seen the place, working there, I'd seen all that shit they have in there? How far out in the brush it was? Burglar alarm didn't mean shit way out there. I knew how to open their gate. I told Crystal, and she said, Well, let's go have a look."

"What did you take?"

"Little kind of safe or like a chest," said Sean. "Steel. Heavy sucker. Crystal'd worked for a guy once had one like it. He kept his coin collection in it. Gold coins. It wasn't, like, bolted down or nothing. We thought we'd toss the place a little bit, fuck it over so nobody would miss the safe right off, take the safe, take the whole fucking thing, and then, later, we had time, get some tools to it, bust it open. See what was in it."

"What was in it?"

"Fuck if I know," said Sean. "We couldn't get into it. Took it back to Crystal's, hid it. Then Saturday we went by her brother's with it. He's got a garage. He's closed weekends. We got out the bars and chisels and shit, sledgehammer, and banged away at it for most of an hour. Fucking nothing."

Sean was laughing now.

"So," he went on, "couple days later, I went out to my uncle Fred's, there in Humber. He's got this big fucking magnum revolver. Told him I needed it to kill a dog, had rabies. Fred is so fucking dumb.

He said sure. I got the revolver and a box of shells, and Crystal and me took the safe and the magnum way out into the woods back of her place, there. Set the safe up on a log. We were going to shoot the fucker open. You know, you see them do it on TV all the time."

"So you do. How did that go for you?"

"Went like fuck-all," said Sean. "*Blam, blam, blam* — we shot up half the box at it. Did nothing. You couldn't even hardly tell where we'd hit it, just little dents and like smears from the jackets on the rounds. Great big fucking .44 magnum, there. They do it on TV all the time, you know? Shoot the lock? Shoot the door open? Bullshit. We couldn't even knock the fucker off the log. Crystal was pissed."

"What then?"

"Crystal said, Fuck it, we'll lose the thing," said Sean. "She told me to drop it off a bridge somewhere."

"Did you?"

"She thinks so."

"Where is it, then?" I asked Sean.

"It's in a safe place, Sheriff," said Sean. He was so stuck on himself.

"That's why I wanted to see you," he went on. "Like you say, those Russians or whatever the fuck? They want their little safe. They want it very fucking bad. Ain't that right?"

"I'd say it was."

"Well, then," said Sean, "I reckon they can pay me for it. What do you reckon?"

I didn't answer him. I sat there looking off over the hills and shaking my head.

"That's why I wanted to talk, see?" Sean said. "You, you're working with those fuckers, ain't you? Investigating for them? You know them. You can make the deal. Tell them to make me an offer. We'll give you a piece."

"We?"

"Me and Crystal."

"I thought Crystal thought you'd got rid of the safe," I said.

"Oh," said Sean. "Oh, yeah. Yeah, she does. Okay, then, I'll give you a piece."

"Going to cut Crystal right out, is that it?" I said. "Being kind of tough on her, ain't you? What's she going to say?"

"Fuck I care?" said Sean. "Fuck her. She ain't the only girl in the world."

"I guess not," I said.

"There's others, Sheriff," said Sean.

" 'Course there are."

"More than one," said Sean.

"Is that right?"

"Fucking-A right that's right, more than one. More than two, Sheriff."

I started the car and got us onto the road headed back down to the Four Corners.

"Where's your vehicle?" I asked Sean.

"Around back of the store," he said. "So, what do you think?"

"About what?"

"About what?" Sean said. "About what we said. About you making the deal. About the plan."

"Oh," I said. "The plan. I think the plan is the dumbest plan since General Custer rode down the hill after the Sioux," I said.

"General who?"

"General Custer. Your great-great-I-don't-know grandfather."

"Oh, yeah?" said Sean. "Well, fuck him, too."

"These people are not going to buy their thing back from you," I told Sean. "What they are going to do, they're going to put your balls in a vise or wire them up to a truck battery, and get you to see things their way."

"Bullshit," said Sean.

"No bullshit," I said. "They can do that. They will do that."

"They can try," said Sean.

"You think you're pretty tough, don't you?"

"Tough enough," said Sean.

"Nowhere near," I said.

"We'll see," said Sean.

"No, we won't," I said.

"Fuck, we won't," said Sean. "Why won't we?"

"Because you won't be here."

"Fuck, I won't," said Sean. "You think I'm going to run?"

"That's right. That's what you're going to do."

"Fuck that," said Sean. "I'd rather they did what you said they'd do to me. I'd rather that than run."

"That ain't your choice," I said. "Your choice is this: You get out of town, now, or you deal with me. Not them. Me."

"Fuck that," said Sean. "You think I'm going to run because you ask me to?"

"I ain't asking," I said.

I left Sean at the Four Corners and went on home for dinner, told Clemmie I'd got delayed at the store, didn't tell her why. Why didn't I tell her? In the kitchen I put her sugar down on the counter.

"What's the matter?" Clemmie asked me.

"Nothing," I said. "Why?"

"I don't know. You look like something's the matter. What's the matter?"

"Nothing's the matter," I said. "When's supper?"

"This side of midnight," said Clemmie. I left her in the kitchen.

Now, I never claimed to be the brightest fellow in the world, but that night I felt like my IQ, such as it was, had lost twenty-five or thirty points just from my sitting for ten minutes in the same car with Sean. What was going to become of him? The way he was going, nothing good. The way he was going, even the bottom of the law wouldn't be the end of his fall.

One thing, though: I guessed I knew where that little strongbox was. I guessed I did. If I was right, then maybe I could let the air out of this business, maybe I could make this business go away — if Superboy would only get to hell on the road.

12

NEGATIVE

Well, he made it, but not by much. Three more minutes, and he would have been too late. Three more minutes, and we would have been into a different kind of game, here.

Tuesday night about ten, I got a mobile call from Trooper Timberlake. He was en route to Sean's parents' place in Afton. Sean was there. He was loading up his truck, getting ready to take off, it looked like. Melrose Tidd had called the state police barracks to turn Sean in. He hadn't called the sheriff's department. The state police dispatcher was putting it out on all bands, though, because Deputy Keen had advised that Sean was wanted for questioning in connection with the shooting in Monterey. Therefore, if you were any kind of peace officer at all, if you had a badge out of a Corn Flakes box, you were on your way to Afton.

I punched it and got there in twenty minutes. Trooper Timberlake was sitting in his patrol car in the dark beside the road at the bottom of Melrose and Ellen's driveway. Nobody else had showed up, not yet.

Timberlake didn't leave his patrol car. I parked the truck behind him and went to his window.

"Is he still here?" I asked Timberlake.

"And a good evening to you, too, Sheriff," said Timberlake. "That's affirmative. He's there. He's in the garage. Him and his mom, both."

"Where is everybody?" I asked. "I thought the place would be crawling."

"It will be," said Timberlake. "But it seems as though the dispatch said *Grafton*, not *Afton*, so some of them had to turn around. They're straight now, though. They'll be here directly."

"Grafton?"

"That's affirmative, Sheriff."

"That ain't even in the county."

"That's affirmative, Sheriff," said Timberlake. "Honest mistake. Happen to anybody. How do you want to do this, here?"

"I want to talk to them alone, before the army, navy, air force, and marines get here," I said. "Can you handle that?"

"I can handle it for about three minutes. That's how long you've got, more or less."

"I'm obliged," I told Timberlake.

"It's your show, Sheriff," said Timberlake. "Call me if you need me. I'll be right here."

"Thanks, Trooper."

"I'll be right here, studying up on my Russian," said Timberlake.

Some of these young hotshots are trying to develop a sense of humor, it looked like, and that's good to see, but I didn't have time to appreciate it right then. I walked up the driveway to the garage. The lights were on inside, and the door was open. I could see Sean putting boxes and bags into the rear of his truck. Ellen was sitting on a kitchen chair watching him. She had a paper tissue balled up in her hand, and she touched her eyes with it from time to time. When I stood in the door of the garage, she left her chair and came to me.

"What do you want, Sheriff?" she asked me. "What do you want with us?"

"You know what I want," I said. I nodded at Sean.

"He's leaving, Sheriff," said Ellen. "He's going away. Are you here to stop him?"

"I won't have to stop him in a couple of minutes," I said. "Half the law in the county's on its way here. They'll stop him."

Sean slammed shut the tailgate of his truck and came to stand behind Ellen.

"I'm out of here," he said. "All I need is five minutes to go over and tear the lungs out of that fucker Melrose."

"Sean . . . ," said Ellen.

"You ain't got five minutes," I told Sean. "If you're going, go now."

"I'm going," said Sean. "I got some people to see first."

"I bet you do," I said. "Go ahead. See them. Long as they ain't here. Long as you ain't here. You're all done here."

"You fucking got that right," said Sean. "There's fucking nothing here, never has been."

"Sean . . . ," said Ellen.

"That's the way we like it," I said.

"Ahh, fuck it," said Sean. But he was going. Did he take time to say goodbye to his mother, to give her a hug? Did he offer to shake my hand, or even turn to look at me? Not Superboy. He got in the truck, started the engine, and rolled out of the garage and down the driveway without lights. He passed Trooper Timberlake's patrol car, but Timberlake stayed in the vehicle. In the road, Sean switched on his lights and drove off.

"Well, Sheriff," said Ellen, "you've done it. I hope you're happy. You've been down on that boy all his life, you've never given him a break, and now you've finally driven him from his home. I hope you're happy now."

I didn't answer her. I was waiting for the others to begin turning up.

"That boy has never been given a break of any kind, by anybody," said Ellen. She shook her head; she touched her damp tissue to her eyes.

"Some people would say different," I said. "Where's Melrose?"

"He's in the house," Ellen said. "This doesn't concern him."

Melrose was going to be sleeping on the couch tonight, it looked like.

"Here they come," I said.

From the door of Melrose and Ellen's garage you could see up and down the road for a quarter mile each way. Now from both directions came blue lights, yellow lights, red lights — the whole Christmas tree. Trooper Timberlake saw them too. He got out of his patrol car, put his state trooper hat carefully on his head, and came up the driveway to stand with Ellen and me in the garage.

First man on deck was Deputy Keen. No surprise there. He came fast from the left, overshot the driveway, braked hard, skidded, reversed at speed, and came up the driveway backward, spitting gravel. Lyle threw his door open, left his patrol car, and came toward the three of us with his sidearm out and ready for business, held in both hands, pointed away but not far away. When he got close enough to see us in the dark, "Sheriff?" he said.

"Put up your weapon, Deputy," I said. "We're secure here."

"Where's Superboy?"

"He don't appear to be on the premises," I said.

"The hell he don't," said Deputy Keen. "His dad called it in. He's here. We can take him."

"That wasn't his dad," said Ellen. "That was my husband, Melrose."

Lyle looked from one to another of us. His mouth was hanging open. He was breathing hard. He still held his pistol two-handed, but now he had it pointed to the ground at his feet.

"His dad's dead," said Ellen.

"War hero," said Trooper Timberlake. How did he know about that?

"So what?" Deputy Keen said. "He's here. He was here."

"Maybe," I said. "He ain't now. Put it up."

"If he ain't, it's because you let him walk," said Lyle. He put his gun away. "You let him walk, because you either can't or won't do your job. Can't or won't. Which is it?"

"You might want to go a little slow, here, Deputy," said Trooper Timberlake. "You're talking to your boss."

"My boss," said Deputy Keen. He practically spat it. He turned on Timberlake. "You were here," Lyle said. "You know what happened. You're in it, too. He let him walk. He let Superboy walk away. He was here, Superboy. You know he was."

Timberlake didn't answer him. He looked at Lyle from under his broad, flat-brimmed trooper hat. Timberlake's a good deal bigger and taller than Lyle. He had five inches to look down at the deputy, and he used all five of them.

"You saw him, didn't you?" Lyle demanded.

Timberlake looked at him.

"Didn't you?" Lyle was practically shouting now.

"Negative," said Trooper Timberlake.

SIX RIGS AT THE ETHAN ALLEN

Six vehicles were in the parking lot of the Ethan Allen Motel when I drove in. I looked for the big Mercedes that Logan Tracy rode in, but it wasn't there.

Six rigs.

Tracy had called that Tuesday, in the afternoon before Sean had taken off. He wanted to meet — it was important. I told him, okay, I could be at the Russians' place up on the mountain in an hour.

"No," said Tracy. "Not the house. I'm in the city. I'll be up there tonight late. I'll meet you someplace else tomorrow. Someplace quiet. Someplace private. Nowhere near the house."

I told him about the Ethan Allen, a big old place on Route 10, right at the county line. It had the reputation of being what they used to call a No-Tell Motel, but it was easy to find. Tracy was driving up from New York that night, he said. I met him about ten the next morning.

Six rigs in the lot at the Ethan Allen.

The Mercedes wasn't there, and neither was Tracy's slab of a driver, unless he was in the motel. He wasn't. I found Tracy's room, knocked on the door. Tracy opened the door a crack and peeked out, saw me, and practically pulled me off my feet into the room. He shut the door and locked it. Inside all the curtains were drawn.

"Sheriff, you have got to find that kid," Tracy started right in.

"Good morning, Mr. Tracy," I said.

"This is not a game, Sheriff," Tracy went on. "You have got to get that safe. I don't mean soon. I mean now."

"Nice to see you again, too, Mr. Tracy."

"Don't try to smoke me, Jack," said Tracy. "You've got as much exposure in this thing as I have."

"Then how come I ain't soiling my britches, like you?" I asked him.

Tracy turned red. I thought for a second he was going to jump me. But then he shook his head. He held up his hand toward me. He nodded. He sat down on the bed.

"Start again," said Tracy.

"Good idea," I said. I waited for him to go on.

Six rigs in that lot.

Tracy rubbed both his hands over his face, roughly, like he was trying to keep himself awake. His eyes were red, and they flew around the room, up, down, and into the corners, like little red birds, trapped. I sat on the room's other bed, facing him. Our knees almost touched between the beds.

Six rigs.

"These are not patient people, Sheriff," Tracy said.

I nodded.

"They send their guys up here after your friend Sean Duke," he said, "and they don't find him, or he gets by them. So what? Do you think they're going to quit? Do you think they're going to say, 'Oh, okay, you win?'"

"I thought you didn't know nothing about that. You said you didn't."

"Come on, Sheriff," said Tracy. "What do you want me to say, here? Yes, I know about the people they sent. I also know they'll send more. They sent one, then two. They'll send five, ten, as many as it takes until they find him."

I nodded. Six rigs out front of the Ethan Allen. That's a funny word, ain't it: *rig*?

"They won't stop there, either," Tracy went on. "They'll go to people they think can help them find him. They'll go to those people's families. There's nothing they won't do. They will go after — Sheriff, they will destroy — anybody who gets in their way, anybody who doesn't help them get what they want. That includes you, Sheriff."

"It includes you, too, don't it?"

"Why do you think I'm here?"

"What's in their strongbox?" I asked Tracy.

"I don't know."

"Who's the fellow was up at the house the other day? Hair slicked down. Didn't have a lot to say for himself. Who's he?"

"I don't know."

"You talk to him, don't you?"

"As little as possible."

"But some. What do you call him?"

"Mr. Smith. I call him Mr. Smith. Help me, Sheriff. Tell me you'll find that kid before they do. For his sake, for yours. For mine."

"I don't see what you've got to be worried about," I told him. "You're their insurance man, ain't you?"

"I'm not performing," said Tracy. "What they want to happen isn't happening. I'm not making it happen. Sheriff? Are you listening, Sheriff?"

Rig. It's an old-fashioned word, ain't it? It means something more like a buggy or a carriage, a horse-drawn outfit, than an outfit with a motor to it. But we call a car or a truck a rig. Six rigs. Six rigs in the lot out there, right now. The people who drove them here were in these rooms, right here, separated by these thin Sheetrock walls, doing what the Ethan Allen was set up to have them do. They were doing it right now.

"Sheriff? Are you hearing me, Sheriff?"

"Say what?"

"There was a guy, my predecessor," said Tracy. "At a firm in the city. He handled things for them."

"For Mr. Smith?"

"That's right," said Tracy. "Something got fouled up, some arrangement they had — I don't know the details. Something they didn't feel went right, on my predecessor's watch. You understand?"

I nodded.

"He and his wife and daughter were driving the girl up to her school in Massachusetts one weekend. They never made it, never got there. They disappeared. All three of them. They were never found. Their remains, their car, their things — nothing. Gone."

I nodded.

"What do you think about that?" Tracy asked me.

"If your daughter goes to school in Massachusetts, put her on the train."

"This is no joke, Sheriff."

"I know it ain't," I said. "But I don't run this kid. Sean. I don't boss him. Suppose I did. Suppose I could find him. What if he don't have their strongbox anymore?"

"Then he's dead."

"What if nobody has it? What if Sean says he couldn't get into it, so he dumped it? Lost it. Threw it in the river."

"Then he's dead. These people want their safe. They don't want a story."

"Then there's more fellows on their way up here to get Sean?"

"Count on it."

"You know who they are?"

"No."

"You know when they're coming?"

"No."

"Can you put me together with Mr. Smith?"

Tracy looked at me. "You want to meet Smith?" he asked.

"That's right."

"Why?"

"I'm going to reason with him."

"You're crazy."

"Can you get him up here?"

"You're kidding yourself," said Tracy. "You have no idea what you're getting into."

"Can you?"

"Maybe," said Tracy.

"Well, then," I said.

I wanted to get done with Mr. Tracy. I wanted not to have to talk to him, not to have to talk to anybody for a minute. I needed a minute. I left Tracy in his room and went out to the truck. I sat in the truck. I rolled the window down, then I rolled it back up. Six rigs in the parking lot at the Ethan Allen. Four of them I didn't know. Two I did. One was Sean's truck. The other rig was Clemmie's.

I sat in the truck. I needed a minute. I knew I had to get out of there, I had to get out of that lot. I started my engine, but I didn't leave the motel. Instead, I found myself backing out of my place, pulling the truck around behind the building, and parking at its end, just at the corner. I could see the lot, but most of the truck was behind the building. I turned off the engine and sat. I watched the parking lot. What was I doing?

What was I doing? I couldn't be here. I started the engine again and was reaching to put the truck in gear when a door opens at the other end of the Ethan Allen, and Clemmie and Sean come out. They might have been a hundred feet from me. Sean goes first, Clemmie a couple of steps behind him. He goes to his truck, climbs in. He rolls the window down. Clemmie's car is parked beside Sean's. She unlocks it and opens the door as Sean starts up, backs out, drives to the lot's exit, and turns left on the highway. He's gone. Just like that. While I'm watching them, Sean and Clemmie don't touch. As far as I can tell, they don't even speak.

Clemmie's standing at the door of her car. For a second, she watches Sean drive off, then she turns to get into her car. She looks over the roof of her car, in my direction. She stops. The sun is in her eyes; she can't see much. Clemmie shades her eyes with her hand and looks across the parking lot, at me. Can she see me, in the truck? No. Can she see the truck? Sure, she can see part of it. Can she tell whose truck it is? Don't know. She gets in her car, starts the engine, and backs out of her place. She heads for the exit. Near the exit she stops, waits. Her backup lights go on. She's going to make sure the truck ain't mine. But what if it is? I know you, Clementine. You don't want to step off the bridge here. Not really. Do you?

Clemmie changes her mind. Her backup lights go off, and she rolls slowly to the exit, turns right, and takes off.

14

THERE SHE WAS

Okay. Alright. Take a minute. What have we got, here?

What have we got? Well, you know what we've got. There she was. There Clemmie was, with Sean, at ten AM in a by-the-hour motel out on the highway. You know what. But, the thing is, questions. Questions come up. Such as, for how long? For months? For years? Is today at the Ethan Allen, maybe, the first time? It might be. And what if it was, would that make a difference? Would anything make a difference?

You have to think it ain't the first time, though, don't you? And then a lot of little things come piling in: looks, things she said, times she wasn't home, times she ran late, times she was at a friend's. Were those times other — were they other times? Some of them? All of them?

And what about those friends? Whose friends? Who knows about this, besides Clemmie and Sean, and now, me? Who don't know about it? Nobody? Everybody? Addison? Beverly? Errol? The ladies in the post office? In the bank? Their cats and dogs? Who's sorry for me and I don't even know it? How big horns has Sean hung on me, here? Spikes? Full rack? Question is: How big of a fool have I been made out to be?

And by Sean? Well, why not? Think about it. Sean needed to see me the other night. He worked it very neat. Well, but Sean ain't neat. But Clemmie is. Sean found me the way he did because Clemmie ran out of sugar and sent me for more. No. Clemmie might run out of salt, but never sugar. Sweet girl that she is.

But Sean? That sad, sad little boy. Well, but he ain't a little boy anymore. No, he isn't, she said. Everybody knows Sean Duke. Everybody? He's a popular young man. He is? He's got a nice mouth. A nice mouth? What does that mean, exactly? He's not my type, she said. He's not? What do you do with the ones that are, then, Clemmie? Clementine. Oh, my darling, oh, my darling, and so on.

Okay. What happens now? The biggest question of all. The question for me. What am I going to do? Now we come down onto the tough one. Not what's Clemmie doing, when, with who — all things I can't do anything about — but what am I going to do? What's my move? Things only I can do anything about.

Well, it looks like you've got a range of choices, from doing nothing to blowing everybody up. As for blowing everybody up, I've seen what happens when people take that road. I've seen it more than once. Blowing everybody up don't always go the way you think it ought to.

For example, years ago we had this fellow Mort, lived over in Dead River Settlement, right the other side of the old bridge, worked at the AO plant in Brattleboro. One morning he starts feeling poorly at work; there's a bug going around. Mort clocks out, comes home at lunchtime. Walks into his house, place is quiet, his wife's not around. Mort's feeling worse and worse, decides he'll lie down. Goes up to the bedroom, opens the door, and here's the wife in the rack with the oil-burner repairman.

Well, Mort's got a temper on him, it looks like. He reckons he'll blow everybody up. He's in shape to do it, too, because he's got a .38 in the nightstand right beside the bed. Thing is, the wife knows it's there, too, and, the situation being the way it is, she's a lot closer to the nightstand than Mort. If she and the oil-burner fellow can get themselves untangled, they can beat Mort to the draw. Mort sees this.

So, not thinking too clearly, he turns around and runs downstairs for his twelve-gauge, grabs it, runs back upstairs, busts into the bedroom to find the oil-burner fellow putting on his pants and no sign of the wife. Mort blasts the oil-burner fellow with the twelve-gauge and gets down on his hands and knees to look under the bed for the wife, going to blast her, too, when here the lady comes jumping out of the closet, stark naked except for the .38. She gives Mort all six, dead center. I mean, she punches his ticket for good, right there.

Mrs. Mort puts her clothes on, calls the police. Well, there's quite a considerable flap, of course, but, upshot is, it's a clear case of self-defense. The oil-burner fellow gives his evidence; he took a couple of pellets, but Mort was wide on him and he recovers okay. He and Mort's wife sell the house and move to Florida. Not Mort, though. Mort's still here.

No, blowing everybody up don't always come out right. Plus, in my case, blowing everybody up would set kind of a poor example in a law enforcement officer, wouldn't it?

So, go to the other end of the range. Do I do nothing? That don't seem possible either, but look at it. It's like sheriffing, ain't it? There's different ways of doing nothing. It makes a difference who knows what. I know what I know. But it makes a difference what Clemmie knows. I saw Clemmie at the Ethan Allen. Did Clemmie see me? I know what I know. Does she know I know? Does she know I know she knows I know? You can give yourself a headache with stuff like this. It is what it is — but what is it?

And then what happens? Last question. Suppose I don't blow everybody up, but we don't do nothing, either. Suppose we break up. How do we do that, exactly? Who breaks, and where to? I'm not talking about furniture and dishes. I'm not even talking about houses, bank accounts. I mean who goes, and where? It ain't like Clemmie and I can go our separate ways. We don't have separate ways. Clemmie's New York mom chucked her marriage to Addison and went home. Clemmie and I can't do that. We can't chuck our marriage and go home. We are home.

Things will change now, they'll have to. But how can they? Well, we'll find out, won't we? And after all, you expect that. You know things will change. You expect the future to be different, more or less. But the past is different, too.

The past is different now. The past has changed. That's what I can't get used to. You expect change in the future, but you reckon the past is set, it's permanent. No, it ain't. The past, my past, our past, is different now. It's different since I spotted Sean and Clemmie at the Ethan Allen. All those years, we haven't been having the life I thought we'd been having. It's as though you thought you were the cavalry and one day you realize you're the Indians. You've been wrong, you've been off about everything, off right from the start. And the start wasn't yesterday, it wasn't last week or last month. We're talking about years, here.

———

The first time I saw Clemmie, that I remember, she was thirteen or fourteen, and she and a bunch of her Brattleboro cousins were hanging around the cold drinks table at Taft's while the bigger kids and Taft and his men made hay. I was working for Taft that summer. I got down from the load we had brought in and went to the table, dry as dust. Taft had the usual drinks in bottles and cans, and he had a big bowl of what the older people called dipper, which Taft made up out of cold spring water, molasses, ginger, and vinegar, and which was supposed to quench your thirst better than anything.

I filled myself up a jar of dipper, and Clemmie, who was standing by watching me, said, "My Lord, are you really going to drink that stuff? You should have a Coke."

"Who says?" I asked her. I drank my dipper.

"I do."

"Who are you?"

"Clementine Jessup."

Clementine Jessup. I can't say I took special notice of her that day. Yes, she was on the pretty side: she had light brown or dark blonde hair and freckles. But a lot of kids have freckles. And yes, she was sassy, but a lot of girls that age are sassy — maybe more are sassy than ain't. I didn't pay much attention at the time. I had other things on my mind, I guess. A couple of weeks after that day at Taft's, I was in Long Beach, then Da Nang. Got done with them and came home, dubbed around, wound up in the state police, as I have told.

So it was five, six years later on another early summer day during my first year as a trooper that I saw Clemmie again. I was patrolling on the river road in Cardiff, a quiet two-lane, just cruising along, when this little VW Beetle comes flying by me on a double line, I mean flying, doing about seventy. For a second I didn't believe it, thought I'd been asleep dreaming: nobody blows out a state police patrol car like that, not unless they've just robbed a bank. But there was the VW, in the distance ahead, getting smaller fast. I lit up and took off after it, pulled it over just at the Gilead line. Walked up to the car, and here's Clemmie, digging her license out of her handbag, her hair in her face, and her summer dress pulled up into her lap on top of about five miles of bare legs.

There she was. Some days in May, June, being a speed cop is the best job in the world.

"I know, I know," Clemmie said when I was standing beside her window. "I was over the speed limit."

"You were over it by about a hundred percent, ma'am," I said. "Didn't you see me? A police car? That was a police car you just passed. You were doing at least seventy when you went by me."

"I was in a hurry," said Clemmie. She handed me her license, and I read the name on it and looked at her again — at her face — to find her doing the same to me.

"I know you," Clemmie said.

"Yes, I guess you do."

"My Lord, Lucian Wing," said Clemmie.

"That's right," I said.

"Where have you been?"

"I've been around."

"No, you haven't."

"Well, I've been in the service."

"I had the biggest crush on you," Clemmie said.

"You did?"

"I did. You were older, though. You were out of school. You didn't know I was alive."

"Sure, I did."

"No, you didn't," said Clemmie. "You didn't then. But you do now."

I gave her her ticket and sent her on her way. We began to see each other here and there, first by chance, then not. Things moved along, I guess, and by and by we began talking about making the business official. We did that, and we also bought our little place here, started getting set up.

One night, when we'd been married a year or less, we were lying there half asleep, talking things over, the way you do, and Clemmie started recalling when she first knew we were into something, the two of us.

"I'd had a crush on you," Clemmie remembered. "But that was nothing. That was years back. I was a little kid then. Later you were away, and later still, you were here and I liked you well enough, I guess, but I didn't think much about it. You were older."

"Older?" I said. "What? Six years?"

"It seemed like a lot then," said Clemmie. "And it was odd, because even though I wasn't all that attracted, wasn't thinking about you all the time or anything like that, still there was something about you that was stuck in my mind and that I couldn't put my finger on. It wasn't anything you did, or said, or any way you looked or didn't look. It was just this thing about you. This question.

"I didn't know what it was," Clemmie went on. "It was like trying to remember something, like a name, and you can't, you can't quite reach it, you can't quite say it. I mean, it drove me nuts. Was it something you'd done that I'd forgotten? Was it something somebody had said about you? Was it that you were funny, or serious, or nice, or not-nice? No, I knew it was nothing like that. I couldn't place it. And then one day — I think I'll always remember this — I hadn't seen you for a couple of days, wasn't thinking about you at all, and I came downstairs in our house and there was Daddy standing on a chair hanging a picture on the wall in the sitting room. He was up on a chair and he was pounding a nail into the wall with a hammer, for the picture. But the chair was uneven, and so was the floor. He was unsteady up there. And I watched him, and I thought, he'd better watch out, he's pretty shaky, he could fall. What if he should fall? He's all alone. And that second, bingo. It came to me, not about Daddy — about you. And I said, My Lord, that's it. That's what it is about Lucian. He's not funny or serious. He's not strong or weak. He's not good or bad. He's not the right guy or the wrong guy. He's my husband."

———

By the time I got back to the department from the Ethan Allen, I'd about decided that, for now, I'd go ahead and work this thing like a job of sheriffing. I'd sit tight and wait for what was going to happen to happen. Then I'd see. "Let it come to you," Wingate said, "whatever it is."

It was a good plan, it usually is, but it didn't work. It didn't have a chance to work. I didn't get to try it. When I got back to the department, I found Beverly had lost contact with Deputy Keen. His patrol car was at the Russians' house, but he wasn't with it. He'd gone missing. Where was he?

15

MORE COSSACKS

They'd found him by the time I got there. He was unconscious and badly busted up, but he was alive, though how long for you didn't know. Deputy Keen looked like he'd walked into the buzz saw. As I pulled in at the Russians' house, the medics had just loaded him into the ambulance when his heart had quit. They had put the electric paddles to him to start him up again, and I found the deputy flopping around in the back of the ambulance like a big bass in the bottom of a rowboat.

There was quite a crowd at the scene. Beverly had put out that an officer was unaccounted for and presumed to be in trouble. So by now the Russians' place was like a law-enforcement zoo, with every kind of cop there is, including a couple of officers of the Royal Canadian Mounted Police who'd been passing through.

I found Trooper Timberlake. He said Buster Mayhew, the Russians' caretaker, had come by to check the house and found Lyle's patrol car there. The door was open, the engine was running. No sign of the deputy. Mayhew had used the radio in the patrol car to call the department — and here we all were.

Deputy Keen had been found quickly, at the end of a blood trail where whoever worked him over had dragged him into the woods maybe a hundred feet from the house. His sidearm was on his belt; so was the rest of his equipment. He had a big gash on his forehead, a broken leg, and possibly a broken neck. Now he was on his way to the emergency room in Brattleboro. If he got there alive, he had a shot, one of the medics said.

Buster Mayhew was standing around a little apart from the others, looking like he'd forgotten why he was there. I went over to him.

"You didn't see him at all, then?" I asked Buster.

"See who?"

"The deputy. Deputy Keen? The one just left in the ambulance?"

"Oh. No, I didn't see nobody."

"Did you look in the house?"

"The house?"

"That's right, the house. This house. The house you caretake. Did you look inside at all, see was anybody around?"

"Oh. No," said Buster. "I mostly take care of the outside, you know."

"Okay," I said. Making good use of Buster was not something that got easier with time, it didn't look like.

I decided to follow the ambulance to Brattleboro, see how Deputy Keen made out. Then, on the way down, here came Beverly on the radio about a disturbance at the trailer park in Monterey, Crystal Finn's place. That made me think of Sean. Was he not taking off, after all? Was he still out in the high grass somewhere? He'd better not be. I turned off and went over to Monterey with the lights going.

———

Sean wasn't there, but he had been, and not long since. His clothes and other belongings were scattered all over the yard in front of the trailer: jeans, shirts, underwear, socks, sweatshirts, caps, a shaving kit, a set of barbells. Crystal Finn had thrown them all out the trailer's door. Then she had kicked some of the clothes into a pile, and now she was on her knees before it with a can of Pabst Blue Ribbon in one hand and a cigarette lighter in the other, trying to set fire to Sean's clothes. She was having a hard time getting it to catch. When I got out of the truck and came over to her, Crystal looked up at me and said, "Oh, fuck, it's you. You got any kerosene?" She was not sober.

"Where's Sean?"

"Not here."

"When did you see him last?"

"About five seconds after he told me how he's been two-timing me with some stuck-up bitch slut whore from Mount Zion."

"You mean Morgan Endor?"

"I don't know her name," said Crystal. "If I did . . ."

I remembered the shotgun Crystal had used on the Cossacks a couple of days ago. I didn't see it. Maybe it was in the trailer. That was fine by me. It looked like Crystal had come down on the opposite end to mine of the range of choices open to the two-timed.

"What happened?" I asked her.

Crystal drank deeply from her beer and nearly tipped over backward. She sat on the ground in front of the pile of Sean's clothes. A thin curl of smoke had begun to rise from the pile where she had been trying to light it.

"What happened?" I asked her again.

"What happened?" she said. "What happened is that that sack of shit, that pig, just got around to telling me he's been sticking it to what's-her-name, in Mount Zion, for four months. Four months."

"Let's get you inside," I said.

"No," said Crystal. "Go away."

"Come on," I said. I got her elbow and started to lift her to her feet.

"No," said Crystal. "Cut it out."

"You'd rather be arrested?"

"For what?"

"Unpermitted burn," I said.

"Fuck you," said Crystal. But she stood up, and with my arm around her waist so she didn't fall, she made it to the trailer.

"Get some sleep," I told her.

"Four months," said Crystal. "Four months he's been porking that whore. Four months. We only been together for six."

"Is he at her place, probably, then?"

"I think I'm going to throw up," said Crystal.

"Go on inside," I said. "You'll be okay."

"I won't be okay," said Crystal. "I'll never be okay."

"I need to know if Sean's in Mount Zion now," I said. "Is he?"

"No, he's gone," said Crystal. "He left. He's gone." She started to cry. "Four months," she said again. "Almost our whole time. It really fucks with your head, you know?"

"It does," I said. "I know."

———

I got Crystal into her trailer, got her laid out on her face on the divan. She went right to sleep. I found a blanket and covered her. Then I remembered her dog. I looked around. The dog was there, alright, sitting in the doorway to Crystal's bedroom, looking straight at me. It was quite an animal: as it sat upright on its haunches, its head was a little above the height of my belt. It let out a low growl. I froze. I kept my eyes on the dog's. Jackson.

"Okay, Jackson," I said. "Okay, now."

This dog had about taken an arm off one of those Russians the other day. But now it didn't offer to move. It cocked its head to one side and gave its tail a wag. It watched me. I watched it. I took a step backward, toward the outside door. I took another.

"Okay, Jackson," I said again.

Jackson stood. He walked over to Crystal, passed out on the divan. He sniffed her face, then he rested his head gently on her back and shifted his eyes to me. He sighed.

"Okay, Jackson," I said. I turned to the door. Crystal's Ithaca was there, leaning against the wall. I broke it down. Then I opened the door and left the trailer, taking the barrels with me.

I went on down to Brattleboro to the hospital. There I found the news was good. Deputy Keen was going to be alright. He was concussed, and his neck had been wrenched. But it wasn't broken, and otherwise he had stabled out. His leg was badly fractured, though, and he had two cracked ribs; he'd be laid up for some weeks. He was awake. I could see him if I didn't stay long.

Deputy Keen lay in his hospital bed. He looked like an exhibit of what the doctors can do for you when they give it everything they've got. He had a big bandage on his head, his middle was taped, he wore a high neck brace, and his left leg, in a cast, was hoisted up on a chain hung from a rack above the bed.

Trooper Timberlake was with him, and so were the two Mounties, big calm fellows who kept telling us they were going to have to get on their way back north and then didn't move.

The deputy was telling his story. There wasn't much to it. He had gotten the idea that the key to this whole business was the Russians' house. He reckoned either Sean or the Russians or all of them would turn up there sooner or later, so he'd been keeping an eye on the place as best he could. That morning, while I was counting rigs at the Ethan Allen, the deputy had been patrolling in Grenada. He'd driven up to the house, and, lo and behold, here was that big Mercedes parked in the drive.

Lyle had stopped his patrol car a little way behind the Mercedes, got out, and started toward it, when the driver's door opened and out climbed maybe the same Russian gorilla I'd seen driving Mr. Smith. Or maybe it wasn't the same gorilla, because a second later the rest of the doors opened and three more gorillas just as big as the first one got out of the car. One of them leaned back into the rear and came out with a baseball bat. The four of them began walking toward Deputy Keen.

Lyle told them to stand where they were, but he didn't know how to say it in Russian, it looks like, so maybe they didn't understand him. In any case, the four gorillas fanned out a little and kept on coming.

Deputy Keen reckoned they were down onto it now, or close enough. He reached to unholster his service pistol — and the lights went out. Somebody must have snuck up on him from behind and sandbagged him. He woke up in the intensive care in Brattleboro.

A nurse came in then and kicked us out. In the hospital parking lot, Trooper Timberlake and I shook hands with the Mounties, and they got back on the road. I went home. I knew I was out of time, here. The business with the Russians had to end. I had to make it end. I was pretty sure I knew how to do that. But I didn't like it. In sheriffing, you don't make things happen. You let them happen. You let them end, if you can. But you can't, not always.

———

It was late before I got home that night. I found Clemmie had gone to bed. That suited me. I went into our bedroom. She had left the light on for me. She lay with her back to my side of the bed, her shoulder uncovered. The strap on her nightgown had slipped down over her upper arm. I looked for a minute at the light brown freckles on her bare shoulder and back. I always liked Clemmie's freckles. In the winter they nearly disappeared, but every summer they came back. They were some of the first things I had seen on her that day at Taft's years ago when she was a kid, when we were both kids, when the only freckles I knew for sure she had were on her face.

I didn't wake her up. I turned the light out and went to the couch in the other room. I undressed and lay down on the couch. I lay on my back. I looked up overhead, where the tilted shadows wheeled and backed across the plaster ceiling as the lights of a car passing in the road came in the dark window. I waited for the next car, the next lights.

Sean had a horse, a big hunter, withers high as your head, a stallion. He was up on it at the edge of the river, on the bank. Sean wanted to ride the stallion into the river and across, but the stallion wouldn't go. Sean was putting his heels to it, and the horse kept balking and pivoting away from the river: it wouldn't go into the water.

I was on the river bank nearby. I was telling Sean he needed to get a blanket or a sack or something of that nature and put it over his stallion's head so it couldn't see the water. Then it would cross alright. Sean didn't know that. He didn't know horses. How would he? He didn't know some horses are afraid of water, moving water, running water. Some horses are afraid of the river.

Wingate was there, too. He stood to one side, also talking to Sean, or maybe he was talking to me. He said, "It's like the difference between ... It's like the difference between ... It's like the difference between ..." He never finished.

Sean kept on spurring the stallion, and the stallion kept on shying and circling and dancing away from the river. Hours passed. More hours. It was never going to end, and then it did. It ended when Clemmie came down the bank, walked to the riverside where we were, took the reins from Sean, and led the stallion into the water and across. Easy as pie. On the other side, she slapped the stallion on its rump, and it galloped off with Sean bouncing up and down on its back. They were gone.

The next morning I was up early. Clemmie was in the kitchen, at the sink. She turned to me as I came in.

"You were late last night," she said.

"I was."

"You slept in the other room."

"I didn't want to wake you."

Clemmie looked at me for a minute. Then she turned back to the sink.

"Are you home for dinner?" she asked me.

"Far as I know," I said. "You?"

"Far as I know."

16

THE STAR

Sean had some people to see, he'd said. I knew who one of those people was, didn't I? Sean had some people to see, and then he had a long road ahead of him — or anyway I hoped he had. I hoped it like fury. The road was there. Let him take it.

Would he be taking it by himself? Clemmie hadn't been ready to step off the bridge yesterday at the Ethan Allen, but she'd stepped onto it. Was she ready now? Well, I'd find out pretty quick. Wouldn't I? I'd find out soon enough, but before I did, I had people to see, myself.

I drove up to Mount Zion about eleven Thursday. Morgan Endor came out the front door of her house and met me on the little porch.

"Sean's not here, Sheriff," she said. "He's gone away."

"I know," I said.

"You do? How? He only left an hour ago. Have you seen him?"

"Not today."

"Did he call you?"

"No."

"Then how do you know he's gone?"

"He's pissed in every corner of the pen. When you do that you find a new pen."

"Do you know where he's going?"

"No."

"I do."

"You think you do."

She smiled and nodded. "You're right," she said. "Won't you come inside, Sheriff?"

She led me through a sitting room and into her kitchen. Her cat was lying on the floor in the sun, but when I came in it got to its feet, stretched, and walked out of the room.

"Sean said you'd probably be stopping by," said Morgan Endor.

"Yes," I said.

"He left something for you."

"I thought he might."

"He left the thing you were asking about."

"Good."

She sat me down at a table and took the chair across from me. We sat facing each other, quite close. I'd guessed wrong about her age the other day, it looked like. I mean, I'd guessed wrong, again. I'd put her around forty, but now I saw there was a good deal of gray in her hair, and her hands were thin and dry. Morgan Endor was no forty: she was looking at fifty, no question, and maybe looking from the wrong side.

"Sheriff?" she said. "Do you hear me?"

"Say what?"

"I said I want you to know Sean only brought it here last night, your thing," she said. "It wasn't here when you came last weekend. I didn't know about it. I wasn't lying to you."

"I never said you were."

"But you thought it," she said. "You thought I was lying to protect Sean. You thought I was in love with Sean. You thought Sean had fucked me until my brains fell out. You thought Sean had fucked me stupid."

"It's been known to happen," I said.

"Not to me," said Morgan Endor.

"No, probably not."

"Would you like to see my work with Sean?"

"You mean your pictures?"

"My pictures, yes."

"Maybe some other time."

"There is no other time, Sheriff," she said. "They'll be packed and shipped over the weekend. The shippers will be here tomorrow, actually. I'm flying out of JFK Monday. Don't you want to see them?"

"I'd rather see the other thing," I said. "The box."

"You can see that, too, Sheriff. You can see everything. Come with me."

We went into a hall and upstairs. The whole second floor of the house was one big room. It was fitted up like a picture gallery, full of light from a row of skylights in the roof, plain white walls, no carpets. Morgan Endor started walking slowly around the room, not speaking, and I followed her. We looked at the pictures hung on the walls. They were hung in a single band around the room, about eye height. Twenty-five or thirty pictures.

I admit when the lady had first told me about taking pictures of Sean, I thought I knew what kind of pictures she was talking about. I was wrong. In each of the pictures Sean was looking straight into the camera, face-on. And in each he was wearing a different get-up, a different costume. Not simple costumes, either. In one Sean was dressed like one of the Three Musketeers, in velvet and lace and carrying a sword and wearing a hat with — what is a big feather they wore in their hats back then? — a hat with a plume. In one he was dressed like a western cowboy. Sean was a judge in a black robe, a priest in a dog collar, a skin diver with a face mask and a spear gun, an old-fashioned gent in a fancy suit and a vest. He was a farmer, a soldier, an astronaut, a Roman gladiator, an ancient

Greek in one of the sheets they wore, a jockey in silks. I mean, there was even a photo of Sean dressed as a lady singer, like a nightclub singer, in a long gown, with makeup, a wig, and a string of pearls. There was one where he was dressed as a policeman.

"That one's for you, Sheriff," said Morgan Endor.

"For me?"

"I'll sell it to you. Of course, you'll have to wait until the show is over."

"The show?"

"The show in Paris, Sheriff. Paris, France? Remember? I told you."

"So you did."

I looked around the room. We had seen all the pictures. We were standing in front of the one of Sean as a cop.

"I'll reserve this one," she said. "The gallery won't sell it. You can have it when the show comes down."

"How much?" I asked.

"Five thousand dollars," said Morgan. "Or, no, we'll say forty-five hundred. Law enforcement discount."

"Out of my range."

"Really? Pity. But, I'm curious, Sheriff. What do you think? What do you see?" She swept her arm around the room.

What did I see? All those pictures, all those clothes. All those different people, all Sean. At first they were funny, more than anything, I guess; then they weren't. Sean was always looking out at you with the same kind of look, no look, like he was having his photo taken at the motor vehicle department for his driver's license. He didn't care what get-up he had on, didn't even know, maybe. Was he having fun? It didn't look that way. Was he pretending to be whatever he was dressed up to be? That would be fun, wouldn't it, for a while anyway? But no, he wasn't. Sean wasn't part of what he was doing. He was the little kid in the graveyard again, in his too-big jacket and his too-long tie, waiting while the grown-ups buried his father.

"What do you see?" Morgan Endor asked again.

"I don't know," I said. "It's always him, ain't it?"

"That's right, Sheriff. It's always Sean. That's why I used him."

I nodded.

"Sean is all inside," she said. "I told you that earlier. He lives inside himself, he never comes outside, he doesn't even know there is such a place as outside himself. That's why he appears the way he does in these images. Wherever you put him, he's always the same. That's what you see."

"That's what *you* see. I see a dumb kid in a bunch of funny clothes you hung on him to play some game of your own."

"You underestimate me, Sheriff," she said. "You certainly under-estimate Sean. What Sean has you can't buy, you can't acquire. He's like an actor, a great actor. Don't you see? Give Sean any part. He's in it, but it's as you say: He's always Sean. You always know him. Sean's a star, Sheriff."

"I don't see it."

"Of course you don't. Do you know why you don't see it?"

"Why?"

"Because you're the same thing — the same as Sean. More than Sean."

"I'm a star?"

"To your fingertips, Sheriff. I'm only sorry it wasn't you who came to fix my roof."

"I ain't."

"We should work together, actually. We should do a series. We really should."

"A series?"

"A series of images, like these," said Morgan Endor. "You'd see what I mean, I promise you, you would. What about it? I'll be back in Vermont next spring."

"I thought you didn't work on old men," I said.

"In your case, Sheriff, I'd consider making an exception. I could take you, Sheriff. I could take you all the way."

"No chance," I said.

"But why not?"

"I can't tell you all the reasons."

"Why can't you?"

"There's too many."

"How many?"

"I'm not an educated man," I told her. "I can't count that high."

She smiled. "You make my point, Sheriff," she said.

"You want to show me what Sean left for me now?" I said.

"Alright, Sheriff."

We went back downstairs and into a little room off the kitchen, a bedroom. On the floor was a steel safe about the size of a case of beer — a bigger thing than I'd have thought. And solid. There were some scars in its finish from the shots Sean and Crystal had fired at it, but them aside, that safe might have been sitting on the shelf in the safe store, brand new. Only Sean would have thought he could get into that thing with a sledgehammer, or with a gun, the way they do on TV.

"There's a note," said Morgan Endor.

It was lying on top of the safe, a piece of lined paper, folded once. I picked it up and opened it.

SHERF LUCIN
HERS YOUR FOKIG BOX. GIVE IT TO

YOUR FUKIG KOMIE SPIKS + TELL
THEM TO STUCK IT. TELL KRISTLL
THT DEPTY IS A PUSY. HA
RESPETFULY
S. DUKE
PS TELL CLAMMY I SAD BI. HA

"Clammy's my wife," I said. "Clemmie."

"I know who Clemmie is."

"She and Sean are friends."

"I know that, too, Sheriff."

"Sean told you?"

"No."

"How do you know, then?"

"Don't worry about Clemmie, Sheriff. She isn't going anywhere."

"She ain't? Ain't she a star, too, like the rest of us?"

"No. She's not."

"She's just the regular thing, then? The straight thing? Is that it?"

"That's it, Sheriff."

"But there's Sean," I said. "What about Sean?"

"What about him? Do you think she wants Sean?"

"I don't know what she wants."

"I do."

"What?"

"You."

"Me? She's got me."

"Maybe she doesn't think so."

Morgan Endor was looking at me. She shook her head. Then

she said, "You're a smart man, Sheriff — as stars go, I mean. You want to open your eyes, though."

"They are open."

She smiled at me.

"You think so, Sheriff?" she asked. She turned and led the way back into her sitting room. I carried the safe. Her cat must have known I was getting ready to leave, because it came into the room, found the patch of sun it had left earlier, and flopped down on the floor.

"What happens to the cat?" I asked Morgan Endor.

"How do you mean, Sheriff?"

"You're leaving. You won't be back till next year. Cat's not going to Paris with you."

"No."

"What do you do about it, then?"

"Nothing," said Morgan Endor. "The cat can take care of itself."

———

I'm a star, the lady said. That's a good thing to be, ain't it, a star? I've been called a lot of things, but that's a new one. Well, it's changing times, ain't it? The way I said before, we've got different kinds of people passing through here from what there used to be. Take the Russians. Take Morgan Endor. People you never do get.

But you can get them partway. The Russians? I get them. They're evildoers. Morgan Endor? Don't know. *I could take you all the way, Sheriff.* I doubt it. I doubt it like hell. But I don't know. And it don't matter, now. Sean's off. Maybe I didn't get Morgan Endor all the way through, or even close, but I got enough. I got more than Sean. (Well, according to what you mean by "got.") With Morgan Endor, Sean was like — what is the insect where in mating the fellow climbs onto the lady and goes right to his work, keeps at it, having a hell of a time, and then when he gets done he finds she's eaten him up from the head down to the shoulders? Like a big, long-necked grasshopper, it is. With Morgan, that was Sean. He thought he was the do-er. He wasn't. He was the do-ee. I wondered if he'd ever figure that out.

And where does Morgan get so smart about Clemmie? Who Clemmie is, what Clemmie's going to do or not do, what Clemmie wants. She don't even know Clemmie. She don't know Clemmie, she don't know me. We don't need some foreigner, some artist, to tell us what we want. We can take care of ourselves, Clemmie and me.

17

EVERYBODY LOVES HONEY

"Well," Wingate said, "that don't help; that don't tell you much, does it? That don't help much, putting it that way."

"That's the way you put it," I said.

"No, it ain't," said Wingate.

We were sitting out back at Wingate's. He had a little yard behind his place in South Cardiff. Wingate didn't get around very well the last couple of years, but he could still mostly take care of himself. He had a visiting nurse who came in every other day, and he had friends who stopped by to lend a hand, or just to visit. I was one of them. I got over to Wingate's every couple of weeks. "Going to Delphi," Addison called it. Good old Addison.

A brook ran at the bottom of Wingate's yard. We sat in a couple of camp chairs set up on the grass and listened to the brook running over its stones and watched Wingate's bees coming and going around their hives. We didn't talk a lot. The older Wingate grew, the less he had to say. When you were with him, you got to be the same way, it looked like.

"How's your deputy?" Wingate asked at last.

"How do you know about that?"

"Nurse Penelope, there, told me."

"You don't miss much, do you?"

"Not much," said Wingate. "I can't. You want to know what's going on, you want to know what's developing, get yourself a visiting nurse. She'll let you know, whether you want her to or not — especially if it's bad."

"He'll be okay, they say. Might take awhile," I said.

"He's a ball of fire, ain't he?" said Wingate. "That deputy."

"You could say that."

"Nurse Penelope said he took on eight, nine men."

"Five. They took him on, more like."

"Still," said Wingate. "That's a coming young fellow, there, ain't he? Injured in the line of duty? He's up for a commendation, they say."

"They say."

"That kind of thing goes good in the papers," said Wingate. "Attracts attention. For a young fellow looking to rise, I mean."

"Yes," I said.

"It looks good to the voters," said Wingate.

"Yes," I said.

"Shows energy," said Wingate. "Shows initiative. Not like your old time-servers, just sit around and let things slide."

"Yes," I said.

"Voters like to see that, initiative."

"Yes," I said.

" 'Course," said Wingate, "it may show initiative, but it don't show a lot of sense, it don't show a lot of smarts, does it, to get into that kind of thing to begin with? Five on one? No backup?"

I didn't answer him. We sat for a while and watched the bees. Wingate had three hives set up in a row at the edge of the woods that went along the brook.

"Not much of a year for honey," said Wingate after a few minutes.

"No?"

"Not really. Haven't had a good year in some time. Cold springs, maybe. Bee diseases. And then, fellow down the road had six hives. Bear came in one night, smashed them all up. Totaled them. He had to start again from scratch."

"Is that right?"

"Now the fellow's put in a big steel fence, an electric fence, around his hives. I saw it. Quite a setup. You don't know if he's running bees or a prison."

"No fence for you, though, I guess?" I said.

"I guess not," said Wingate. "I don't like them."

"Ain't you afraid the same bear will come down the mountain one night and get your hives?"

"No, I ain't. No bear will try it on around my place."

"Why not?"

"I'm the sheriff."

"You're retired."

"Bear don't know that."

"Do you remember that fellow Mort?" I asked. "Over here in Dead River?"

"Shot by his missus?" said Wingate.

"That one."

"Sure, I remember him," said Wingate. "Hard to forget a thing like that, ain't it?"

"How do you do something like that?" I asked.

"Nothing to it," said Wingate. "You point the gun. You pull the trigger. Gun goes bang. You've done it."

"I don't mean her," I said. "I mean him. Mort. He was ready to blow them both up. He tried to do it, too. How do you do that? How do you get there?"

"You lose it, it looks like," said Wingate.

"But how? How do you lose it?"

Wingate shook his head.

"'Course," I said, "some people would say he was right, Mort. Some did say it."

"Some people will say anything," said Wingate. "It ain't right if you're dead."

"No."

"Nothing develops, nothing gets better if you're dead. You're alive, things can get better."

"They can also get worse."

Wingate shrugged. "Well . . ."

"Tough to come home and find her like that, with some fellow," I said.

"Sure, it's tough," said Wingate. "But people are going to do what they're going to do, it looks like. You can't stop them. You shouldn't try. That's where you get in trouble."

"Mort thought he could stop them," I said.

"Be hard to prove he was right, though, wouldn't it?" said Wingate. "With the way things developed."

Now a cat came walking into Wingate's yard from the left, not sneaking around, but walking stiff-legged, almost strutting. It passed near the beehives, slowed down, looked at us, and went on across and out of the yard. We had a good crop of cats, here and there, that summer, no question.

"Whose cat?" I asked Wingate.

"Next door's," said Wingate. "He comes through every day about now. He'd like to get to the hives, too, but he knows what would happen if he tried."

"What would happen?"

"He'd get stung."

"Oh," I said. "I thought you meant you'd get after him some way."

"No," said Wingate. "There ain't much I could do to him. The bees can take care of themselves."

"Except for if it's a bear," I said.

"Well, yes. Except for then," said Wingate.

"Or a cold spring, or bee diseases," I said.

Wingate nodded.

"I didn't know a cat would go for honey," I said.

"Everybody loves honey," said Wingate.

We sat without talking for some little time.

"Nurse Penelope said she heard, she understood it was out-of-staters busted up your deputy, there," said Wingate.

"They're Russians," I said.

"That's out of state, ain't it?"

"It is."

"They're a pretty rank outfit, I guess," said Wingate.

"They are."

"What are you going to do about them?"

"I'm going to make them go away," I said.

"How are you going to do that?"

"I'm going to reason with them," I said.

"Same way you reasoned with the Duke boy?"

"Sean?"

"That one. He was mixed up in that thing, wasn't he? What happened with him?"

"That nurse keeps you right up to speed, don't she?"

"I told you."

"I cut him loose."

"You did?"

"That's right. He's moved on."

"I thought he broke into their place up on the Gold Coast," said Wingate.

"He did."

"And you cut him loose?"

"I did."

"Why would you do that?"

"I don't know why."

"I do," said Wingate. "It's in the Bible. Fellow's a shepherd, fellow has a hundred sheep. One goes missing. What does he do? He goes after the one, leaves the other ninety-nine. Good luck to them. They can take care of themselves. Does that make sense? Well, no, it don't. Not really. The value's in the ninety-nine, ain't it? Not in the one. You write off the one. That makes sense. What the Bible fellow did don't make sense, but he did it anyway. Everybody does."

"Is that why?"

"Why what?"

"Why I cut Sean loose?"

"That's one reason, ain't it?"

"There's another?"

"There's always another," said Wingate.

He leaned forward in his chair and rested his elbows on his knees. He looked out across the yard, past the beehives, and into the woods.

"I used to tell you," he said, "you deputies? Years ago? I used to say, 'You go out as wise as serpents and as harmless as doves.'"

"I remember. That's the Bible again, ain't it?"

"You bet."

"You're all over the Bible today, ain't you?"

"Nurse Penelope's a lay reader," said Wingate.

"I might have known."

"You've about got the dove part down, it looks like," said Wingate. "You might need to work on the serpent part."

"No, I don't," I said. "I got that part down, too. Plus, the serpent part ain't sheriffing."

"It ain't?"

"No. People are going to do what they're going to do."

"Well," Wingate said, "but that don't tell you too much, does it? That don't help much, putting it that way."

"That's the way you put it," I said.

"No," said Wingate. "I put it that you were to do the job. Never mind how it sounds later, when you say it right out — just do it at the time you've got it to do. Do your job. I put it that way. Do the job."

"But you didn't say what the job was."

"Didn't I?" Wingate asked.

"Not that I recall."

"If I didn't," said Wingate, "it's because I didn't have to. You knew."

"What did I know?"

"People are going to do what they're going to do," said Wingate. "You can't stop them. You get out of their way. Then you come in with the mop and the bucket."

"That's what I said, ain't it?"

We sat. The same cat came into the yard from the way it had left by a minute earlier. It walked across the yard in front of us, disappeared.

"How's Clementine?" asked Wingate.

"She's good," I said.

—— 18 ——

ANOTHER WORLD

Deputy Keen got his Governor's Public Safety Award for Distinguished Service in Protecting the People of the State at two in the afternoon Monday. They made quite a thing of it. The ceremony took place in Lyle's hospital room, where there was packed in enough brass to open a candlestick factory. The lieutenant governor was there, the state's attorney general, both state senators from our county, the head of the hospital's board of trustees, Lyle's surgeon, the assistant surgeon, a couple of nurses, two press photographers, and — lo and behold — Crystal Finn, looking like the new young minister's wife, her hair washed and pinned up, wearing a pretty blue dress with sleeves down to her elbows so you couldn't see her snake. Lyle lay there in his bed having his picture taken and shaking everybody's hand, flashing a big grin. His busted leg was hauled up in the air, making him look like he was trying to kick the moon.

After the ceremony, when people were starting to leave, I went over to the bed to say goodbye, when, "Stick around, Sheriff," said Lyle. "Come back in ten minutes."

So I went and got a cup of coffee and brought it back to the deputy's room. Everybody had left but Crystal. She was sitting on the bed next to Lyle. When I came in, she gave him a big kiss, picked up his hand, and held it in her lap.

"We're engaged," said Lyle.

"Yes," I said. "I guess you are."

"When I saw how she ran off those weasels with that old Ithaca, I knew she was the girl for me," said Lyle.

Crystal giggled and patted his hand.

"Yes, sir," said Lyle. Then he looked up at Crystal and squeezed her hand. "Give us a minute, sweetheart," he said.

Crystal got up from the bed and left the room. Lyle and I watched her go. She was a well-put-together girl, no question.

"Sit down, Sheriff," said Deputy Keen. I sat. He reached to the table beside his bed and picked up the award he'd just been given, a framed certificate with ribbons and seals. He looked at it and dropped it on the bed.

"Bunch of crap, ain't it?" the deputy said.

"Not all of it," I said.

"Thanks," said the deputy. "Thanks, but you know different. I just got a medal for being coldcocked like the dumbest drunk in the bar. That's a bunch of crap."

I didn't say anything.

"I'll take it, though," said the deputy. "I'd be a fool not to."

I nodded.

"Here's the thing, Sheriff," said the deputy. "I don't know how to say it but to say it. I want your job."

I nodded.

"I'm coming after you in the fall. The election. I'm going to run against you."

"I thought you might be," I said.

"I want you to know it ain't personal," said Lyle. "You're a good man, you've been a good sheriff. But it's another world we're in now from the one you came up in."

"It is?"

"You know it is. The ways you learned don't work any more. They for damned sure don't work on them Russians. They don't even work on the locals. Look at Superboy."

"What about him?"

"He's a criminal. He has been for years. He belongs in jail. But you won't put him there. You keep waiting for him to shape up. We had him cold the other night, but you let him walk. You and that trooper. Where is he now?"

"Traveling."

"Traveling to someplace where somebody else will have to put him in jail. Because you punted. You know I'm right. Admit it."

"I don't know you're wrong. I'll admit that."

"And then them Russians. You keep tiptoeing around them. They're the enemy, Sheriff. We are at war. They are our enemies."

"Suppose you believe that," I asked him. "What would you do?"

"I'd ride them out of town on a fucking rail," said Lyle. "And when they fell off, I'd shoot them."

"Is that right?"

"You bet that's right," said Lyle. "You? You do this job like you're some kind of a social worker. You don't use your departmental vehicle, you drive around in that old wreck. You don't carry your service weapon. You don't even wear a uniform. Do you think people like the Russians, people like Superboy, respect somebody like that?"

"Old wreck? You insulting my rig, now?"

"Do you, Sheriff?"

"I don't care if they respect me," I said. "I care that they do what I want them to do."

"Which is?"

"Leave us alone."

"Well then, you're out of luck again, Sheriff," said Lyle. "Because they ain't going to. No way they are. They ain't going to leave us alone. They're coming in here like a wave of snakes. They don't respect you, they don't respect other people, they don't respect the law. They're coming. They're already here, others are on the way, and we've got to have something more to put up against them than a nice man with a long memory and good intentions."

"Nice man? You calling me a nice man, now?"

Lyle grinned. He shook his head. "Yeah," he said, "I guess I am."

"That 'more' you're talking about," I said. "That 'more' we need to have? That 'more' would be you, I guess."

"Your damn straight right it is," said Lyle.

"Maybe so," I said. "We'll see. But I ain't going to roll over for you, you know. There's an election in the fall — that's unless you've got a better way of doing that, too. Do you?"

"No."

"Well then," I said, "good luck to the both of us."

———

"He's what?" said Clemmie. She was sitting on the couch watching the news on television. "He's what?" She switched off the television.

"He's running," I said. "He wants to be sheriff."

"You're joking."

"No, I'm not. Neither is Lyle. He's running in the fall."

"I don't believe it," said Clemmie.

"Why not? Lyle's a good officer. He's been with the department, I don't know, five, six years. He's a hard worker. He's got this new commendation. He'll make it look like I ain't up to the job anymore. He believes it, too. He'll make others believe it. I don't know. Maybe he's right."

"Right?" said Clemmie. "Lyle Keen? My Lord, Lyle Keen's not a third the man you are. He wouldn't be a third the sheriff you are."

Whoa. What had Clemmie been smoking? It must have been

good stuff to make her talk like that. I'd been looking at her back for the best part of a week. I decided I'd fly one close in front of her stand, see what she did.

"He'll say I'm soft on evildoers," I said. "Like Sean."

Clemmie looked at me. "Sean?" she said.

"He'll say I let Sean get away."

"Did you?"

"Yes."

"Why?"

"Different reasons."

"What reasons?" Clemmie was looking right into my eyes. It made me think how she didn't do that very often.

"We need to talk, don't we?" I said.

"I should say we do," said Clemmie. "I hope he doesn't think he can just announce he's replacing you, not after all the years you've put in. We have to fight this. We need a plan. We need a campaign. I'm going to call Daddy. He knows about this kind of thing."

Clemmie bounced to her feet and took off for the telephone. She left me looking at where she'd been, wondering what had happened to the one I'd flown by her. Had she shot it down? Had she missed it? Had she never seen it? I didn't know.

I did know that by bedtime that night, I had two things I'd never had before — an opponent and a campaign manager — and a third thing I'd had, but not for a while: a wife who was looking at me.

And I didn't sleep on the couch, either.

19

A STUDENT OF HUMAN NATURE

There was another Russian now, a new one. You had to say that for them: they had depth on the bench. And each of them more important than the one before. With the Russians, it looked like the higher you went, the higher you got. But this new one was as far as I was going. If this one had a boss, I wouldn't be meeting him.

I drove up to their house on the mountain with their strongbox in the bed of the truck. I got there about sundown, the sky in the west flaring and flaming like a burning city on the Gilead hills.

The Mercedes was at the door, and as I parked behind it the Russians' big driver got out and came to meet me. He beckoned me to get out of the truck. When I did, he patted me down and nodded toward the door. Then he went around to the rear of the truck, picked up the strongbox as though it were a loaf of bread, and followed me into the house.

In the office or study where we'd met before, the Russian with the slicked-down hair, the Russian who'd never said a word, the Russian Tracy called Mr. Smith, was waiting. He was standing beside the desk. The new Russian was sitting behind the desk. When I came in he got up and went over to the window. He was a tiny old fellow, not much more than five feet high, with a dark brown, wrinkled face that looked like a windfall apple the deer have missed and you find in the long grass under the tree the next spring. He stood and looked out the window at the sunset. Then he turned and came back to the desk.

Mr. Smith nodded toward the desk, and the driver set the strongbox down on it. He stepped back and stood with his hands clasped in front of him. Mr. Smith, the little fellow, the driver, and I stood there and looked at the box on the desk. The numbers weren't in my favor, were they? Three Russians, one the size of a tree, and myself. They had me if they wanted me, it looked like; but at least they were wearing all their clothes.

Mr. Smith said something to the driver in Russian, and the driver said something back. Then Smith nodded again, and the driver left the room. Smith turned to me.

"Please, sit down, Sheriff," he said.

I didn't. I said, "Where's Tracy?"

"Mr. Tracy is no longer in our employ."

"Who's he?" I asked, meaning the little fellow.

"He is our director," said Mr. Smith.

"Who are you?"

"I am the translator."

Mr. Smith talked like a professor, and he had an accent, but it was more like an Englishman's accent than what you think a Russian's would be: *trahns-LAY-tor, die-rec-tor.*

"What's his name?" I asked Mr. Smith.

Mr. Smith spoke to the little brown man, who said something in return.

"The director says you ask a good many questions," said Mr. Smith, "for a man in your position."

"What is my position?"

Mr. Smith passed that on to the director. The director shrugged his shoulders. He had the damndest outfit on: a one-piece suit that zipped up the front, like a mechanic's monkey suit, but made of some soft, tan, fuzzy stuff. He looked like a pimp on his day off. He said something to Mr. Smith.

"He says you are not armed. Why are you not armed?"

"If I'd brought a gun, you would have taken it away from me," I said. "What would that have proved?"

Mr. Smith translated that for the director, who smiled and nodded and came to the desk, where he sat in the desk chair. It was a big chair; I doubt his feet reached the floor. He had the strongbox at his right elbow. He said something to Mr. Smith. Smith took hold of the strongbox, turned it on the desk so it faced the director, and stepped back. The director took a key out of a pocket in his suit and unlocked the box. He opened it. He looked at me. Then he looked into the box. He took something out of the box; I couldn't see what it was. He looked at it, looked at me again, nodded, shut the box, locked it. Then he laid his hand on the top of the box and said something to Mr. Smith.

"The director asks, do you know who stole this?" Mr. Smith said.

"Yes," I said.

"Who?"

"A kid. A boy."

Mr. Smith translated. The director answered him.

"Why?" Smith asked me.

"He thought there was money in it."

Mr. Smith translated. The director didn't say anything for a minute. Then he asked Mr. Smith another question.

"The director asks, do you know this boy?" Smith asked.

"Yes."

"Do you know where he is now?"

"No."

"But he is here? He is in this district?"

"No."

Now the director spoke to Mr. Smith for a longer time.

"The director says if the boy broke in here and stole this safe, then he is a criminal."

"That's right, too," I said.

"You are an officer of the law. You know this criminal. The director wants to know why have you not arrested this criminal. Is he your son?"

"I don't have a son."

"Is he the son of your brother?"

"I don't have a brother."

Mr. Smith translated that for the little director, who asked a question back.

"Why protect him, then, this boy, this criminal?" Mr. Smith asked me.

"Because that's the way I work."

Mr. Smith translated that for the director. The director looked at me. He raised his eyebrows. He spoke to Mr. Smith.

"That is the way you work?" said Mr. Smith. "The director asks why you work that way."

"That's how I was taught."

"The director asks who taught you."

"Nobody you'd know."

"The director asks," said Mr. Smith.

"I don't guess that's the director's business," I said.

"The director decides that," said Mr. Smith.

"No, he don't," I said. "You've got what you wanted. You've got your box. What do you care who took it or what happens to him?"

"We do not care," said Mr. Smith. "The director is curious, however. The director is a student of human nature."

"I bet he is," I said.

The director was talking again. He said something to Mr. Smith. Then he pointed to the strongbox with his forefinger, his thumb raised, and went, "*Poum, poum.*"

"The director says the thief seems to have shot at the safe," said Mr. Smith.

"He seems to have."

"Why did he do that?"

"He thought he could shoot it open," I said.

Mr. Smith translated. The director answered.

"Why did he think that?" Mr. Smith asked me.

"He saw somebody do it on TV."

Mr. Smith told that to the director. The director laughed. He shook his head. He spoke to Mr. Smith.

"The director says this boy is a fool," said Mr. Smith.

"He is."

"He is a fool, as well as a criminal."

"Right, again," I said.

"The director says he is lucky," said Mr. Smith. "He is lucky he could not open the safe. He is lucky to be a fool."

I nodded.

"The director says if this boy had opened our safe, he would not be a fool any longer," said Mr. Smith.

"I know it," I said.

"He would have been educated by now," said Mr. Smith.

"I know it."

The director pointed to the strongbox and went "*Poum, poum*" again, laughing. He was having a fine time. He said something to Mr. Smith.

"The director says God loves a fool," said Mr. Smith.

"I wouldn't know about that," I said.

The director was talking again. "The director wants to know, what is your office?" Mr. Smith said. "Are you the chief of police?"

"I'm the sheriff," I said. Smith translated that for the director, who asked another question.

"Sheriff of what?" Smith asked me. "The town?"

"County sheriff," I said. "Seventeen towns."

Smith told the director that. The director laughed. He pointed out the window and said something to Mr. Smith. Smith laughed, too. He turned to me.

"The director says you are the sheriff of seventeen towns with no people in them," he said.

I looked at him. The director went on.

"He says it must be easy being sheriff of seventeen towns where there are no people, and where if there were and any of them misbehaved, you would not arrest them because that is the way you work," said Mr. Smith. "It is easy, is it not?"

"Sometimes it is. Sometimes it ain't."

The director said something else to Mr. Smith.

"The director says he would enjoy being sheriff here," said Mr. Smith. "How does one get the job?"

"One's elected," I said.

"The director asks, how it would be if he ran for election to be the sheriff? Would he get any votes?"

"Sure, he would," I said. Mr. Smith translated for the director.

The director had quite a bit to say to that. When he had finished, "The director doubts it," said Mr. Smith. "He says he doubts he could get more votes than you. The director says you're a very good sheriff."

I waited.

"You're a good sheriff because you don't do anything," said Mr. Smith.

The director laughed again. He got to his feet. He said something to Mr. Smith that Smith didn't translate. Then he walked out of the room. From the rear, in his suit, he looked like a little brown bunny rabbit.

"You are free to go, Sheriff," said Mr. Smith.

"I ain't done," I said.

"Yes?"

"You got your box," I said. "Now you and the little fellow and the driver and the whole lot of you — you get out of of my county. Get out of my county, get out of my state. Find someplace else. I don't want to see you, or hear about you being around here again, ever."

"But, Sheriff," said Mr. Smith. "We have a valuable property, here."

"Sell it."

"You misunderstand us, Sheriff," said Mr. Smith. "We are the injured party here, after all. It is we who were robbed. All we want in your district is a quiet life in the country. That is all. The director, as you will have observed, is not young. He loves it here. It reminds him of the country where he grew up. The hills. The forests. The little villages, little churches. So charming."

"Real charming," I said.

"We admire it. We appreciate it. You see, Sheriff? You do not understand us."

"I ain't a student of human nature."

"We are not bad people, Sheriff."

"The hell you ain't," I said.

20

THERE SHE WAS (AGAIN)

You have heard the old joke about the fellow in one of these little towns up here who runs for selectman and loses. The morning after Election Day he goes to the post office and the store, the way he does every day, and all his neighbors gather around. They feel bad for him. They come up to him, and they all say, "I voted for you, wish you'd won," and "It's a damn shame, you should have won. I want you to know I voted for you," and "Well, Bob, you got my vote. Wish it had been enough," and so on. The loser finishes up at the post office and the store, and as he's driving home, he realizes that, if all the people had voted for him who said they had, he wouldn't have lost.

By the fall, when the election was a couple of weeks off, I began to feel like I was getting ready to be that candidate: everybody likes him, everybody votes for him, but the other fellow wins.

Deputy Keen, fully recovered, famous, and back on duty, was running hard for my job. Funny thing was, we were working together and getting along better than ever. Partly that was because Lyle was campaigning a lot of the time, so we didn't see much of each other at the department. But when we did, he was respectful, he was cooperative, he followed orders without giving you his ideas about them. He was nice as pie — kind of like the way the fox is nice to the chicken he knows he's going to be eating before too long.

Lyle had a good campaign going, and he had helpers. Letters started turning up in the newspaper from his supporters. They all said about the same thing: time for a change, time for a new man, new thinking. The present sheriff's a good old fellow, but he's so far over the hill he ain't in the same state any more. He's gotten lazy. Look at how he gives known evildoers a free pass. There was a letter from Emory O'Connor. Emory said how we can't keep our communities safe today using the methods of 1950. I thought that was pretty good.

"That jerk wasn't alive in 1950," said Clemmie.

"Neither were you," I told her.

Lyle wasn't the only one with helpers, of course. I had helpers of my own. Clemmie and her father took the whole business in hand. Did they need me, really? Maybe not: it was for sure my own ideas on how to go about running for sheriff (something I had, on my own, done successfully seven times) came in last in the decision making.

For example, campaign signs. Lyle had them: red, white, and blue cardboard placards that said KEEN FOR SHERIFF. They were stapled to wooden stakes that you drove into the lawn in front of your house so everybody would know who you were going to vote for.

I didn't like those signs. I didn't see why everybody needed to know who everybody else was voting for. Just go vote, was my idea. Forget the advertising. I had gotten elected seven times without campaign signs, and I let Clemmie and Addison know this time wasn't going to be any different.

Yes, it was.

"You've got to have signs, don't you know, Lucian," said Addison. "I'm sorry if you don't like them, but you've got to have them."

"Why?" I asked him. "I've run seven times. I've never had those signs. Why's this time different?"

"You've run seven times unopposed," said Addison. "Now you've got to beat Lyle Keen. That's a difference, wouldn't you say?"

"Daddy's right," said Clemmie.

So we got a couple of hundred WING FOR SHERIFF signs. Ours were green, because Lyle had beaten us to the red, white, and blue. I refused to chase around the county handing them out to voters, though, so Clemmie and Addison took that on, and there is where we almost hit the ditch.

The week before Election Day, Deputy Keen arrested Addison for driving under the influence. Addison had been passing out my signs up in Afton; though how many of them could he have placed at two o'clock in the morning going over eighty miles an hour?

"This is Lyle Keen trying to derail us," said Clemmie.

"Doing pretty good with it, too," I said. "Fellow's running for your job, a law-enforcement job, busts your campaign manager for drunk driving a week before the election. It don't look good. It don't help."

"He doesn't drink as much as he did," said Clemmie. "He was set up. I know he was."

"He was doing eighty-one," I said. "If he don't drink like he did, it's because he's about topped up."

That was probably the wrong thing to say.

"Whose side are you on in this?" Clemmie asked me. "He was trying to help you, you know?"

"I didn't ask for his help."

"Of course you didn't. Mister Law. You don't ask for anybody's help. That's the thing."

"What thing?"

"You know what thing."

"What thing?"

Well, we'd gone about as far as we could go down that road, it looked like. I spent the night on the couch. Next morning, there was Clemmie's back, reared up in front of me like a mountainside, once again.

This was not Addison's first round as a drunk driver. He lost his license for ninety days. Therefore we began to see a lot more of him than we were used to, because either Clemmie or I had to drive him.

"I'm sorry about this," Addison said to me one day when I was taking him to his office.

"Don't worry about it," I said. "It's three months. Anybody can do anything for three months."

"It's going to cut into your margin, though," said Addison. "We wanted a landslide, don't you know, Clemmie and I."

"What are you talking about, margin? What margin?"

"Your winning margin."

"I ain't going to win."

"Of course you'll win," said Addison.

"You think."

"I know. Do you imagine the voters really want a bird dog like Keen for sheriff? Nonsense. All he does is run around arresting people. That's not what anybody wants. Nobody will vote for that. People may say they will, but they won't. You'll see. Keen doesn't understand the job."

Addison was starting to sound like Wingate.

"We'll see," I said.

"Besides," Addison went on. "Do you think I would have agreed to manage your campaign if you were going to lose? What do you take me for, Lucian?"

———

It wasn't all politics that fall, though. From time to time I could still hear the echo of our old business with Sean and the Russians — and I could still count the rigs at the Ethan Allen, although they were starting to fade. Six rigs, five rigs, four, three . . . none. They faded. Should I let them fade? Could I? What was the strong thing to do? What was the hard thing to do? What was the right thing to do? Were they the same? I always thought they were, except for sometimes in sheriffing.

Then on Monday, the day before the election, an envelope came into the department addressed to me by name and with a French stamp on it. Inside was a fancy card that read:

Les Întérieurs Mâles
Photographies Americaines
par
MORGAN ENDOR
Galerie Faye
6 Rue Dauphine
Paris VIème

The card unfolded. When you opened it up, there was the photo of Sean in a frogman outfit: tanks, flippers, speargun. He was staring at you from behind his diver's mask.

I thought I'd throw the card away. Then I thought I wouldn't. I sat behind my desk for a good while. I looked out my window. You could see across the town green to the county courthouse behind the big old maple trees planted in front of it. You could see Leo Crocker raking up the fallen leaves under the trees. Leo had been a year ahead of me in school. First baseman, and could bat left- or right-handed. Leo had a daughter in the air force. You can have a daughter in the air force now. Leo's mother and my mother had been friends. In fact, they had been cousins, so Leo and I were cousins, too, I guess.

Sheriffing was what I knew; it was about all I knew. But what was sheriffing? I thought sheriffing was the real thing: it was getting the job done the best way you could, Monday, then Tuesday, then Wednesday, and all week long. Sheriffing was soft, it was never perfect, but the job got done. The law was different. The law was hard. Clemmie said I think I'm the law. Mister Law, she said. I'm not the law. Far from it. I'm the sheriff. The law was almost the opposite of sheriffing; it was what you got to when sheriffing failed. Sheriffing wasn't perfect, but the law was. It had to be. The law didn't get the job done; it put an end to the job. The law was always there. You could always come to it. Maybe we had come to it here. I put Morgan Endor's card in my pocket.

I took it home with me that night. Clemmie was in the kitchen getting dinner. I handed her the envelope and watched her take out the card. I watched her read the front of the card. I watched her open it to the inside. I didn't say a word. Let's get this done, I thought. It is what it is. This ain't sheriffing anymore.

Clemmie looked at the photo of Sean.

"Oh," she said.

"You know who that is?" I asked her.

Clemmie touched the photo with her fingertips.

"I know," she said.

"We have to talk, don't we?" I said.

Clemmie took her fingers from the photo of Sean and, stepping close to me, she laid them on my lips.

"No, we don't," said Clemmie.

There she was.

I beat Lyle the next day, beat him pretty smart. The week after the election, he took a job with the police force in a town in Massachusetts. He and Crystal moved down there. I understand he's doing very well.

THE NEW MALE AND THE END

The Russians' place burned up in the middle of the night a couple of days before Thanksgiving. It went with a roar: you could see the fire from twenty miles off.

We had been on our way to bed when the squawker went. Clemmie was brushing out her hair.

"You aren't going up there?" she asked me.

"I think I will," I said. I started getting dressed again.

"Whatever for? It's a fire. Are you a firefighter? My Lord, are you a firefighter now, too?"

"No," I said. "I ain't a firefighter. Don't wait up."

"Be careful," said Clemmie.

"Always," I said.

Up on the mountain I found what looked like half the fire trucks in the county pulled in — half the trucks and three quarters of the firefighters. They had gone to a second alarm and then a third, though less to put out the fire than to make sure nobody missed the show. The flames were still going up above the tops of the trees. The flames lit the big red fire trucks and the shiny black and yellow suits of the firefighters, and they made shadows and sparks and red and black smoke. In the night, the place was like hell with the lights out.

I found the Grenada fire chief standing with his crew. The Russians' house was in his town, so he was in charge. He was an old hand.

"Hello, Lucian," the chief said. "Bring your weenies?"

"Just the one," I said.

"Me, too," said the chief. "Least, I think I brought it. It's under here somewhere." He patted the front of the long fireproof coat he wore.

"Quite a blaze," I said.

"You should have been here half an hour ago."

"Anybody inside?"

"I hope not."

"Electrical, or what do you think?" I asked the chief.

He laughed. "This was no short," he said. "Nothing burns like that without help."

"No."

"You were up here a lot this summer," the chief said. "We have to get word to the owner. You know who that is?"

"I understand the place has been on the market."

"Not anymore," said the chief.

"O'Connor's, in Manchester, manages it," I said. "Or, they did this summer. You can talk to them. Emory O'Connor. You know him?"

"I know Emory," said the chief. "Somebody else can talk to Emory."

"There's a caretaker," I said. "Mayhew. Buster Mayhew. You know him?'

"Sure, I know Buster," said the chief. "He was here earlier. I told him to go on home. He didn't have a lot of light to shed."

"No."

"Truth is, Buster ain't the sharpest knife in the drawer," said the chief.

"Well, well," I said, "we can't all be mental giants like me and you, Chief."

"Ain't that a fact?" said the Grenada chief.

I started walking around among the groups of firefighters from the different departments, looking for Buster Mayhew. I didn't find him, but I did find Trooper Timberlake.

"Evening, Sheriff," said Timberlake.

"Trooper," I said. "You see all your friends at these things, don't you?"

"That's affirmative, Sheriff."

"There ain't going to be a lot left of this place, is there?"

"I wouldn't call it a great loss though, Sheriff," said Timberlake.

"Maybe not."

"Sheriff?"

"Trooper?"

"I haven't seen you since the election," said Timberlake. "I wanted to congratulate you. Some of us were pulling for you, you know. 'Course, we couldn't say anything."

" 'Course not."

"And, it's true, some thought Lyle would do a better job."

"Lyle's a good man."

"Yes, he is," said Trooper Timberlake. "Too good, it might be."

"Too good?"

"That's right, Sheriff. You know what I mean."

"I've wondered about something, Trooper," I said.

"What's that, Sheriff?"

"The night Sean Duke took off, when your dispatch sent everybody to hell and gone off to Grafton, should have been Afton? You remember that?"

"I remember."

"How did that come about, how did that develop exactly, Trooper?"

"It seems as though there was something in the nature of a miscommunication, there, I guess, Sheriff."

"You didn't have any part in that miscommunication, I don't suppose?" I said. "You, personally?"

"Well, Sheriff," said Timberlake, "it's possible I might have corrected dispatch's initial transmission in a way that was misleading to some. The transmission was pretty garbled, Sheriff."

"I bet it was."

"Things were developing pretty fast that night, if you recall," said Timberlake.

"I recall," I said.

We stood and watched the Russians' house burn. There must have been some kind of tank or gas line inside, because the flames were higher now than they had been when I drove in. One of the fire companies had its pumper going and was putting water on the ground around the fire. For ten, fifteen feet back, the ground steamed.

"Have you hired a new deputy yet, Sheriff?" Trooper Timberlake asked me after a minute.

"Not yet," I said. "I ain't in a hurry. I'm waiting for the right man."

"That's smart, Sheriff."

"It ain't anything you'd be interested in at all, I don't suppose, is it, Trooper? That deputy job?"

"I don't know, Sheriff," said Timberlake. "It might be. It would mean a pay cut, I guess."

"You guess right," I told him. "I ain't got the governor behind me, you know."

" 'Course not."

"On the other hand, money ain't everything," I said.

"It ain't nothing, either," said Timberlake.

"You're a married man, I think, ain't you, Trooper?"

"That's affirmative, Sheriff. Going on two years."

"Kids?"

"Not yet."

"You'll get by," I said. "You never know. You might take to sher-iffing. It ain't like where you are now. Sheriffing and the state police are different."

"Yes," said Timberlake.

"It's like the difference between a gentle breeze and Hurricane Hugo," I said.

"Yes," said Timberlake.

"Sheriffing's the gentle breeze."

"Yes," said Timberlake.

"It's like the difference between being a fellow in a bear suit, and being a bear."

"Which is which on that one, Sheriff?"

"I'm damned if I know."

"Well, I'll think it over," said Timberlake.

"There ain't a sword in the shop," I said.

"What's that, Sheriff?"

"Nothing. You think it over, Trooper."

"I will," said Timberlake. "I'll get back to you."

———

Clemmie was sleeping when I got home, but when I came into our room she woke, rolled over, and turned on the light. She lay in the bed, looking at me.

"What time is it?" Clemmie asked.

"About half past two."

"What happened?"

"Nothing," I said. "Place is a total loss. Whatever it was up there, it's all over now. It's all gone."

Clemmie yawned and stretched herself. She was still partly asleep. I started getting undressed.

"That was the place you had Daddy find out about," said Clemmie.

"That's right," I said. I was taking off my shoes.

"The place with the Russians," said Clemmie.

"Same place."

"The place with that guy that Sean — that guy that got beaten up."

"The nude male," I said. I was unbuttoning my shirt.

"I remember," Clemmie said. "I thought it was the *new* male. On the radio. I thought the radio said the *new* male."

"Not new," I said. "Nude."

"That's right," said Clemmie. "And you said you were the new male. I didn't get it."

"But you do now." I was unbuckling my belt.

"I guess I do," said Clemmie. "You were joking."

"I was."

"You aren't the new male."

"No."

"You aren't the nude male, either, are you?" Clemmie asked.

"Give me a minute," I said.

ACKNOWLEDGMENTS

It is a pleasure to acknowledge the contributions to *All That I Have* of its principal editors, Chip Fleischer and Roland Pease of Steerforth Press. They have understood the book as well as, and sometimes better than, its author, and their responses and suggestions, through several readings, have been a model of editorial intelligence and tact.